HEKATE

HEKATE

THE WITCH

NIKITA GILL

SIMON & SCHUSTER

London · New York · Amsterdam/Antwerp · Sydney/Melbourne · Toronto · New Delhi

First published in Great Britain by Simon & Schuster UK Ltd, 2025

1 3 5 7 9 10 8 6 4 2

Simon & Schuster UK Ltd
1st Floor
222 Gray's Inn Road
London WC1X 8HB

Simon & Schuster Australia, Sydney
Simon & Schuster India, New Delhi

www.simonandschuster.co.uk
www.simonandschuster.com.au
www.simonandschuster.co.in

The authorised representative in the EEA is Simon & Schuster Netherlands BV,
Herculesplein 96, 3584 AA Utrecht, Netherlands. info@simonandschuster.nl

Simon & Schuster strongly believes in freedom of expression and stands against
censorship in all its forms. For more information, visit BooksBelong.com

A CIP catalogue record for this book is available from the British Library

Hardback ISBN: 978-1-3985-3714-9
Trade Paperback ISBN: 978-1-3985-3715-6
eBook ISBN: 978-1-3985-3716-3
Audio ISBN: 978-1-3985-3717-0

Typeset in Perpetua by M Rules
Printed and Bound in the UK using 100% Renewable Electricity at CPI Group (UK) Ltd

*For you who
is still searching.
I hope you find
what you are looking for.*

REALMS
OF THE
NIGHT

FALLS
OF THE
NIGHT

ELYSIAN FIELDS

CYPRESS
TREE

PALACE
OF
HADES

ORCHARDS
OF
HADES

RIVER LETHE

STYGIAN MARSH

KRONOS'
CAVES

CERBERUS

GATE
OF
HADES

RIVER STYX

MOUTH
OF THE
UNDERWORLD

THANATOS'
PALACE

FOREST OF SILENCE

ASPHODEL
MEADOWS

RIVER MNEMOSYNE

RIVER PHLEGETHON

HEKATE'S
FIRST
PALACE

TARTARUS

RIVER KOKYTOS

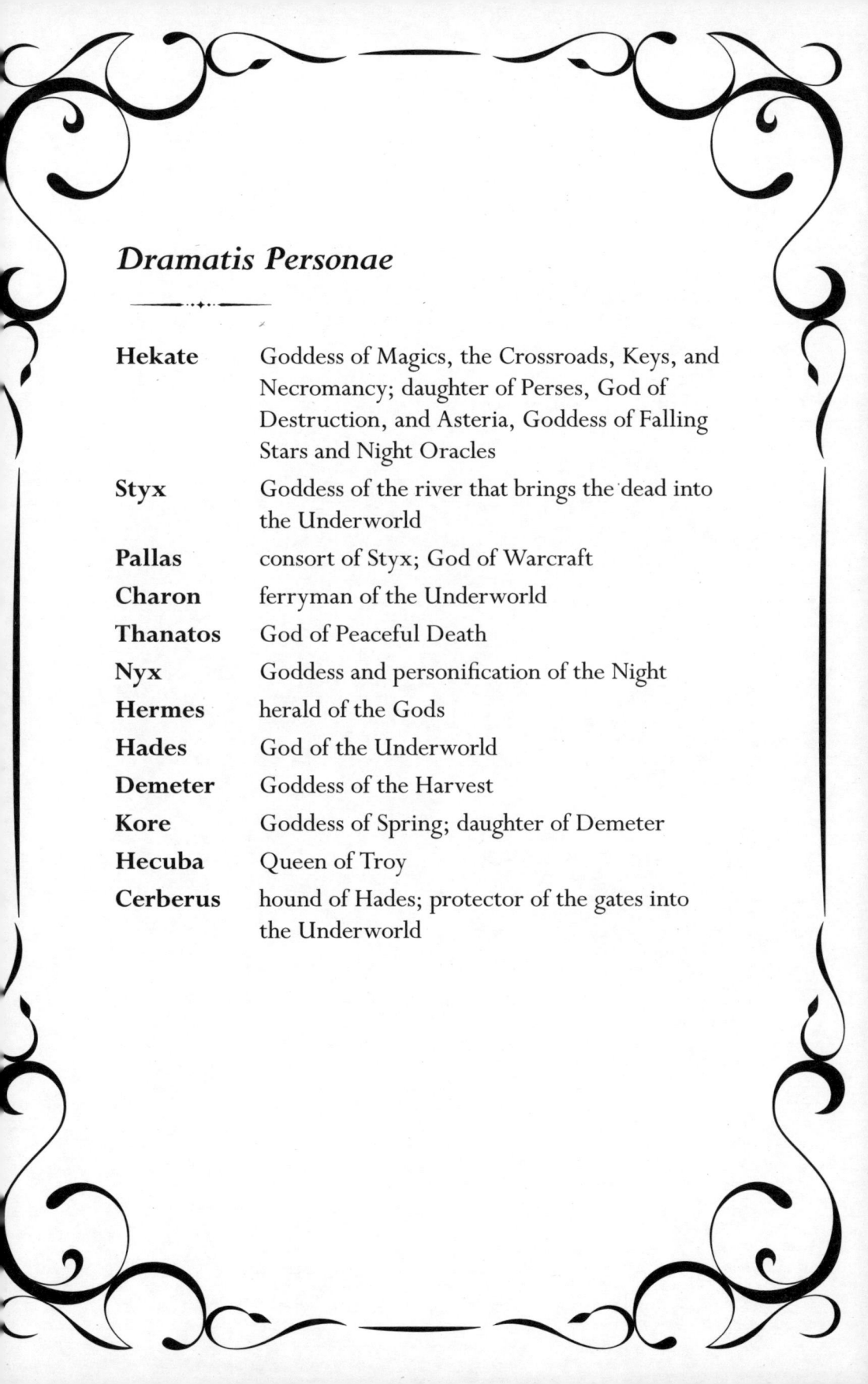

Dramatis Personae

Hekate   Goddess of Magics, the Crossroads, Keys, and Necromancy; daughter of Perses, God of Destruction, and Asteria, Goddess of Falling Stars and Night Oracles

Styx   Goddess of the river that brings the dead into the Underworld

Pallas   consort of Styx; God of Warcraft

Charon   ferryman of the Underworld

Thanatos   God of Peaceful Death

Nyx   Goddess and personification of the Night

Hermes   herald of the Gods

Hades   God of the Underworld

Demeter   Goddess of the Harvest

Kore   Goddess of Spring; daughter of Demeter

Hecuba   Queen of Troy

Cerberus   hound of Hades; protector of the gates into the Underworld

The Titanomachy

A ten-thousand-year war erupts within the most ancient family in the universe: the old Gods, the Titans and the new Gods, the Olympians. Son takes arms against father, cousin fights cousin.

The stakes are impossibly high.

The Gods that win, win control of the entire universe.

The Gods that lose face eternal imprisonment, their powers diminished, brutalized forever.

Prologue

This is an ancient story written long before us.

It is a tale full of Gods and monsters,
divine wars and ghosts,
a tangled mess made
by the divine and the mortal,
mothers and daughters,
the sacred and the courageous,
wounds both healed and unhealed
and the grief that grows
in the absence of love.
There is joy and friendship too,
homegrown and pieced together
by careful, gentle fingers.

At the heart of this story
is a girl looking for answers.

At the soul of this story
is the divine Goddess within us all.

A CHILD OF WAR

•• • ••

PART ONE

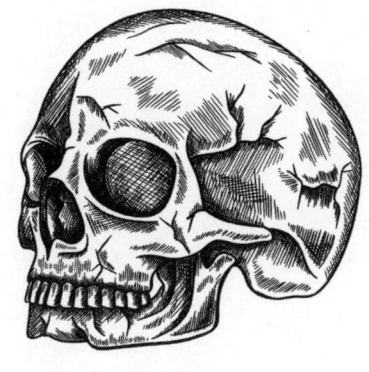

The Day I Was Born

The universe was on fire.
And the reason for this burning
was a family at war with itself.

They called it the Titanomachy.
The war between the old Gods
and the brand new.

Brother against brother,
sisters torn apart,
fathers fighting their children.

And what place does an infant
have among such bloodshed,
such divine terror?

They say on Earth that *ichor*,
the Gods' golden blood,
rained from the sky.

They say that forests
turned from emerald green
to gilded with God-blood.

No one knows
how to stop a war
when you are immortal.

Which is why the universe burned
and as far as the eye can see
there were only embers. And ash.

Mother

was the Goddess of Oracles
and Falling Stars.
On the night I was born
she was all alone.

Her cries were heard by no one
as she drew me wailing
out of her womb,
wrapping me in her arms.

A thousand stars fell
together from the cosmos.
Some called it an omen,
others called it a blessing.

My mother knew better.
Her immortal body already
healed after the birth,
she carried me to

the balcony of her chambers.
As she held me in her arms
we watched a silver shower
rain across the midnight sky

behind the blazing fire
of a ten-thousand-year-old war.
She told me the stars fell

because she had granted
a thousand wishes in my name.

Father

was a God of Destruction.

Ancient and unbroken,
stronger than the core of the cosmos.
The most legendary of the Gods.

And this is why the new Gods
wiped out the stories about him.
A story is a powerful thing.

It can lead to another war
or even resurrect the strongest
of all your enemies.

He was a God so formidable
that the Titans knew no one
but he could win them this war.

My mother said she never believed
any different about my father.
She told me he had never lost

a game of dice, let alone a battle.
I was too young to understand this then.
But sometimes we tell ourselves

the most beautiful lies
just to survive the terrible things
that we are living through.

Home

Children born in wars
are made of a different kind of clay.
We become used to the din.
We grow used to the collapse
of crumbling buildings
and fire and develop a compassion
for broken things.
How can we not when we know
nothing else?

My mother raised me
in a palace where the marble floors
cracked under
the distant clash of God weapons,
adamantine against adamantine.
The cloud-coloured pillars
that held our home up
were disintegrating from the roars
of the heavens above us.

I was told these hallowed halls were
once visited by a thousand giggling nymphs
and hundreds of glittering deities.
But now it was just a haunting
where only my mother and I lived.
When the call to war came,
the Gods, my uncles and cousins, left.
Eventually everyone had to pick a side.
Most of the Titans chose to support my father:
it was after all the Titan God-King
Kronos who they served.
But some Titans betrayed their own.
They took up arms against us,

choosing to side
with Kronos' children,
the Olympians.
The new Gods.

The Children of Gods

are born into deathless eternity.
Our fathers hold us up to the light
and bless us with our purpose as babes.

Our paths are chosen for us
long before we are even conceived,
but at my birth my father was long gone,

fighting a war so far away
he wasn't even there to watch his first child
take her first steps into this world.

My mother told me,
'You are special, my daughter,
which is why you must find your own purpose.

You are no ordinary child.
You are destined for greater things.
A path you must carve alone.

You are not yet a Goddess, Hekate.
That is a divinity you must seek.
And you will find it one day for yourself.'

I think that even then,
she knew what would become of us.
I think she had foreseen the end.

That Last Day

when it was just me and my mother
in behind those crumbling walls,
we found solace in a hidden garden
still untouched by burning ichor.
This secret sanctuary was full of herbs
both magical and mortal.
But my mother's prize
was her soft grey moly flowers.

Legend will tell you that the moly herb
is what Odysseus used to protect himself
from my cousin Circe's magics.
But it was here, in my mother's garden,
that the first sapling of magical moly grew.
It was once a plant grown
only by Goddesses of Prophecy.
It smelt like a mix of lavender and rain.

I can still picture my mother's face
as she took mortar and pestle,
ground the leaves into nectar
and gave it to me to drink.
'I promise you
it will make you strong.
Stronger than anyone
Or anything that you see.'

I would drink the sweet
lavender-honey-rain drink
every time she gave it to me.
I once asked her,
'Why do I need such strength?'
But she turned away

to hide the tears
that fell silently.

When the Messenger Arrived

the sound of his broken wings echoed
across this dilapidated palace.
When she saw him,
my mother *knew.*

He wore my father's sigil
and when we rushed to help him,
he put his hand up to stop us,
his body crumpling to the floor.

We reached him just as
his bloodied mouth opened,
as the ichor from his wounds
pooled at his feet.

'All
is lost.
They are on their way.
You must *run!*'

In the Blink of an Eye

everything changed.
My mother,
who was usually serene,
was suddenly a mask of despair.

She ran into her chambers
and I followed her as she took
a bag and filled it with
herbs and simples, draughts and—

'Mother, what are you doing?!
What has happened?!'
I was only a child as yet.
I had grown quickly from an infant

as all immortal children did,
but I was still too young
to understand what was happening.
My mother did not answer me.

I did notice something
that made my heart pound.
No matter how hard I tried,
I could not hear the din.

The noise of the war . . . *was gone.*

My mother ran towards me
and knelt before me.
'Hekate, you must be brave.
We need to leave.

There are wolves at our door.'

Chased by Wolves

Run

My mother wrapped me
up against her body.

Run

A loud roar and a thud
at our doors.

Run

Barefoot, my mother
rushed to the window.

Run

Just as we heard the doors
thunderously crash down.

Run

And as my mother leapt
from the window

Run

our home turned to rubble
under thudding feet behind us.

Run

When I opened my eyes
I saw what was chasing us.

Run

It was not wolves.
It was two men.

No.
Two hungry Gods.

The Earth After War

Cocooned in the nest of a disintegrating but safe palace, I did not know what the world outside looked like. But my mother, who had grown up playing in meadows and rivers and the ocean with her sister, Leto, and her cousins the Oceanids, knew this Earth well. As she carried me in an ivory cloth slung across her front, all I could hear was her fast-paced heartbeat. She had told me stories about her girlhood, but this Earth had no verdant pastures or vibrant forests like she described. Instead, God-blood still potent sizzled on fertile brown earth and coated dying trees – I could see none of the beauty from her stories here. My mother had brought nectar for us both, but as I grew hungrier for it, my stomach aching with want and then need, I noticed she gave more and more of her share to me. It was only when I saw the sapphire seas like sprinkled diamonds glistening with sunlight that I understood the beauty of the world. But it was fleeting, for my mother cradled me close and summoned the clouds to carry us from one island to the next. Her footsteps, running, made the birds scatter, but where she would have once stopped to soothe them, now she simply kept going. Behind us I heard the thundering chase. What else could we do but run with two hungry God-wolves hunting us down?

At the End of the World

We searched a thousand different homes,
a thousand different islands
and found nothing but ash at each one.

My grandparents' once-grand palace
was now left in rubble and rust,
not a trace of them to be seen.

My mother sobbed at the sight
of her childhood home,
telling her the worst was true:

that my mother's family, the Titans,
once Gods and Goddesses themselves,
had been enslaved by the new Gods,

taken by their own brothers and sisters,
and all that was left were crumbling ruins
just like our own.

With each disappointment, my mother's shoulders
sagged and finally she had to let me
run alongside her on my own.

Once we used to rule everything.
Now there was no refuge anywhere
for old Gods like us, not anymore.

The Last Place Left

Where would you hide
if you were being
pursued by
two of the most powerful Gods?

Where would you hide
if you had already run
through the entire world
and still, still they chased you down?

You would go to the only place
where Gods were not allowed
to enter without invitation.
A place I had been taught to fear.

As my mother stood at
the mouth of the Underworld,
I buried my head
into her chest in fright.

But she was determined,
and she entered the obscure cave,
her feet careful over the rocks
that surrounded the riverbed.

I could hear the running water
of the legendary river the dead took
to enter this cave. But before my mother
could take us further inside,

a figure stopped her in the dark.

The Ferryman

He was a child of Nyx and Erebus,
The Night and the Dark, two of the oldest Gods.
It had been rumoured for a long time
that the ferryman, above all things, was kind.

For to lead the mortal dead was no easy task,
and yet the ferryman did it
without calling it a burden,
without demanding more than what was asked.

But while he had patience for mortals,
it was his own kind that made him wary,
and at the mouth of the Underworld,
it was his boat that stopped us from entering.

'Asteria, you must go no further,'
he warned, but his voice was not unkind.
'Turn back and be on your way; this is no place
for a Goddess and her child.'

My mother, however, was a determined woman
and spoke carefully.
'Charon. It is Zeus and Poseidon that chase us,
they wish to enslave us.

And no, they do not care that Hekate is just a child.'
Charon looked at me, his face stormy,
a sea-God long forgotten.
Then something softened in his ancient eyes.

Without another word, he unblocked our path
and let us pass into the darkness.

Into the Underworld

We were so tired, our clothes were in ruins.
We resembled less a Goddess and her Godling
and more a pair of mortals, bruised and broken feet,

thin from lack of nectar and ambrosia.
I could count my mother's ribs and the angles
of her face now sharp like a knife.

Pain wasn't normal to Gods,
we did not naturally feel it often
and we were able to heal quickly,

but how could you heal when you were running
for your life without a moment's rest?
When we were far enough inside,

we stopped running and my mother fell
to her knees beside the river,
praying, praying, *praying*.

Until, finally, the waters parted
and the River Goddess
rose up out of the depths before us.

The River Goddess

Styx came to us with fangs at the ready,
wet green hair in tangles down to her waist,

her skin so white it looked like
the underbelly of a dead shark I once saw.

Her eyes were pale as bones,
split irises like a snake's,

and when she spoke,
her voice was hoarse.

She said so coldly to my mother
that I shivered at her tone,

'Immortals are not welcome here, Asteria,
even with just cause.'

Tears streamed down my mother's face and, still kneeling, she
grasped my hand.

'Zeus and Poseidon wish us great harm, Styx.
You are the only family we have left.

Please. Do you not remember how once
we had named each other sister and friend?'

Styx's mouth curled but her split eyes softened.
'I cannot help you, even if I wanted to.'

My mother's head dropped into her hands
as a sob escaped her throat,

but then she lifted her eyes with fresh hope.
'If not me, can you take your niece, Hekate?'

Fear

I stared at my mother's hunger-sharpened face
and then back at the cold, fanged Goddess
that stood before us.

My voice was small, desperate and scared.
'Mother, please don't leave me.
You can't leave me *here*!'

Without breaking eye contact
with Styx, she took my hand
and squeezed it and said,

'Hush, my love,
my only child.
Let your aunt speak.'

The Answer

Styx's hesitation was so long,
I furiously blinked tears from my eyes
and stared down at my bloodied
and bruised feet.

I wanted her to say no;
at least that way
whatever happened to my mother,
we were together.

Styx's voice broke through my thoughts.
Quietly and cautiously
she said,

'Yes.'
My mother looked up hopefully,
just as Styx added,
'If Hades agrees.'

The God of the Underworld

His name acted as a summoning.
Before my mother could rise
he was already before us.
Hades of spirits.
Hades of death.
Hades, king of
this strange realm.

The whispers said that
Zeus, Poseidon and Hades,
the three Olympian brothers,
had a choice between the realms
of the sky, the sea and the Underworld.
And Hades chose this place,
where nothing shines
and nothing grows.

My eyes widened when I saw him.
He was more of a boy-God!
Long dark hair tied in a braid,
he wore no crown
and simple dark robes.
His eyes were dark but kind
and his soft mouth looked like
it knew at least a few smiles.
He looked at my mother
and spoke with authority,
his young voice echoing.
'Titanide, this is no place
For immortals that do not
know the ways of the dead.'

Asteria, Titan Queen

I had never seen my mother
beg anyone for anything.

For as long as I had known her,
she carried herself with an elegance,

sometimes even an arrogance.
No one could do what she did:

whisper divine secrets to prophets,
give cryptic tales to Oracles,

tell the stars when it was time for them to die,
showing them their way through the skies.

She invented ancient herbs like moly
that one day became legendary.

I remembered her laughter,
cascading rainfall after a drought.

It was said that Asteria was a Goddess
of such elusive things that other Titans

held her in great respect and with fear
of what they did not know she could do.

But that day she looked so small.
When I remembered my mother,

I tried not to picture that day,
but it was burned into my mind.

The moment she said,
'Please take my daughter.

Give her a place here.
Remember, she is your blood too.'

Hades and Styx

The hesitation was there in both their faces.
Styx's too-sharp eyebrows were furrowed,

Hades' cool dark eyes harboured wariness.
A resounding crack and roar rose behind us.

Hades and Styx looked in its direction sharply,
then back at us as I flinched, my mother very still.

That was the sound of two angry Gods,
enraged at being denied entry to claim us.

Finally, the God-King of the Underworld
gazed at the River Goddess as his mouth set,

A quiet pact exchanged between them.
Then he reached out for my hand and said,

'You have my word, Goddess.
We will keep her safe.'

'Goodbye, My Child. Have Courage'

If I could go back and change anything,
it would be the last time my mother and I spoke.

I would have held her hand a little tighter.
Smiled into her eyes a little longer.

Told her how very much I loved her
and thanked her for what I knew now.

But I was too young to appreciate her sacrifice.
So instead, I looked at my hands

as she got up to leave
and simply wept as she pulled me close.

Then her warmth left me and she walked away
while I screamed and cried and tried

to chase after her as she left in the direction
of the roars and cracks.

Styx and Hades caught me
and held me back.

And as I struggled against their strong grip,
I cursed that I was only a Godling,

I had no powers, I was no Goddess yet.
All I could do was watch as her form

grew smaller and smaller until it disappeared
into the light at the mouth of the cave

that brought us here.

Endings

No one teaches you how to prepare
when you are a child of war.

One day your mother is with you.
The next she is gone.

We do not get safety and
stability. Both are snatched

at the whims of men and Gods.

A New Home

I was my mother's flower child,
the one who helped her grow moly
and visit an open pyre

where we would build a small fire
and she would play with the smoke,
swirl it till it became messages

she would give to her waiting Oracles.
Her careful craft was hypnotic,
and there in the garden

with the distant sound of birds.
I thought it would be my life forever.
Between green grass and blue skies,

the sound of the sea so close by.
Here I was so far under the earth
I could only see the roots of trees.

I once ate fruit from
orchards that belonged to us.
Nothing grew underground.

Because nothing could grow
where everything came to die.
I was hungry and I was expected now

to name this dead place *home*.

In Those First Few Days

Styx did not speak much to me.
I asked her where my uncle Pallas was.
She told me her husband was out hunting
and would not return for a while.

Then she told me never to touch
the water within her river if I wanted to keep my voice, for her
     waters
were known to destroy immortal voices.

Hades vanished after my mother left,
back to his godly duties towards his realm.
So I kept myself occupied by the banks
of Styx, among the skeletons

and skulls of what were once mortals,
who now lay on these riverbanks,
long forgotten and long dead.
I had only lived five years.

And this was how my new childhood
began – full of warnings and old bones.

Abandonment

On the third day of sitting on the banks
I began to think all was lost
and that I had been cast aside
and forgotten.

That now that my mother had left
no one else would ever speak to me.
And talking to the dead was pointless
because what could they even say to help?

I was a lost child.
Perhaps I belonged
nowhere now. Not even here.
Perhaps that was why it happened.

Why the spirit-filled water
of the river began to beckon me.
It asked me to come closer,
for it had a tale I would like to hear.

The whispers filled the cave,
persistent, soft, like invisible hands
pulling me towards the edge.
And I covered my ears

but their voices still filtered in.
If you touch the water,
if you drink from it,
we can tell you where your mother is.

As the voices grew louder,
so did my misery.
My very bones felt tired,
and my head felt heavy.

I wanted to lie down,
to rest a little.
But the coarse earth
of the riverbank

and the chilly darkness
of the Underworld
was no match for my warm, soft bed
made of goose feathers at home.

So instead, I stood up, hesitant,
telling myself it was just a peek.
A small look into the river
to see who was calling to me.

As I approached the river water,
the voices rose in an excited crescendo.
I knelt inches away from it
and saw nothing but my own reflection.

My hand rose from my side
and reached for the water,
but before the river could grasp me
my whole body was dragged away

from the edge.

'What Are You Doing?!'

an angry, familiar voice asked,
as I fell unceremoniously backward
onto the ground.

I looked up to see the ferryman's face,
his dark eyes blazing with fury,
his hand still clenched around my wrist.

But before I could answer
his voice rose again.
'No Godling has ever drank from that river

and lived to tell the tale!'

A Ferocious Rage Emerged

I wrenched myself free of his grasp
and glared at Charon
with burning hot fire in my body.

I wanted to scream
            And scream
                    And scream.

'They know where my mother is!
None of you are helping me!
They want to help me!'

Charon sighed. 'They do not, child.
The spirits lie. That is what they do.
Did no one tell you this?'

I stared at him as though
he had three heads.
'What is a lie?'

Charon rubbed his forehead
and then sat down on the riverbed,
patting the ground to show
he wanted me to sit
down next to him.

I wanted to hold my anger longer,
but my curiosity won
and instead, I sat down.
Charon told me gently,
'You are now a child
of the Underworld.

There are rules here, Hekate.
All things here have a purpose.
Not every purpose is good.'

He took my hand and said kindly,
'Promise me you will not
listen to the spirits again.'

My rage turned into a tearful lump
inside my throat at his kindness.
I nodded, unable to speak.

But what he said about purpose . . .
It reminded me I had none.
Neither good nor bad.
It was true, after all.
A God without a purpose
has no uses in any realm.
That was why it was so essential

to know why we existed,
to know what we were made for.

I Wanted to Weep

but I did not.
Since my mother left,
it felt like she took
my tears with her.

Instead, I looked Charon in the eye,
the hand not in his was shaking
with rage or sorrow,
I no longer knew which one.

'What would you tell a Godling
that has never had
a purpose? What if she is the God
of nothing? Would she matter at all?'

A Lesson

Charon let go of my hand
and I let it fall to my side,
refusing to break his gaze.

Close now, I saw that he
was not as old as I thought.
But then Gods do not age like mortals.

He could have been twenty,
or centuries old, and I would be
none the wiser. He said gently,

'You must see this differently, child.
For you are one of the fortunate ones.
I know it is unusual to be without purpose.

But clearly Chaos,
mother to all us divine beings,
trusts you so well that you

are destined to build your own
path in this realm and the next.
You will learn who you are.

Rely on no parent or God-King
for your eternal gifts.
This is a blessing too, if you see it.'

'How Do You Build Your Own Path?'

I asked him,
my eyes full of wonder
at this thought.

He smiled and it was then
I noticed he was holding
a small golden chalice.

He held it out to me
and said, 'Drink this. It will heal
the wounds of your long travels.'

I flinched at his words.
My travels, which involved my mother.
My mother who was no longer here.

But my thirst overcame me.
Any thoughts were removed
by the delicious scent.

I reached out and lifted the chalice to my lips,
and the sweet, immortal nectar
filled everything wounded within me.

It tasted like honey and home.
It tasted of life and lavender.
Instantly, the voices from the water

disappeared and my head cleared.
I was able to stand
on my own two feet.

I handed Charon the empty chalice
and wiped my mouth
with the back of my hand.

'Thank you,'
I said quietly,
but even as I did,

he was already making his leave.
Charon paused, his back to me,
long coiled hair looking like the river.

'To become a Goddess,
you must first find what
nourishes you forever.'

Styx's Visit

Styx was as strange as her river. She finally returned two days after Charon's gift of nectar. It had made me feel stronger than I had felt in days, weeks, months, but I craved more, much more than a small chalice. When Styx arrived she rose from the spirit-filled water. Her long green hair lay soaked to her waist and when the ghostly hands tried to pull her back, a snake-like hiss escaped her lips, causing them to disperse quickly in fright. I wished to be so terrifying one day that monsters and ghosts were afraid of me. Her fangs glittered as she smiled at me. It was a cold smile, but I had been alone long enough that any interaction with another one of my kind felt like a blessing. She put her hands forward and from the air, it seemed, a silver bowl and a chalice appeared, and she handed both to me.

I Took What Was Offered

recognizing the honeyed notes of nectar, the delicious aroma of ambrosia, food of the Gods themselves. Towards the end Mother was not able to get enough ambrosia, so she began to give all her share to me. As I grew stronger, she weakened. I stared now at the food and drink and wondered where she was and if she had found safety. Styx gestured to the food, as if to say *drink, eat*. I devoured the nectar and ambrosia she gave me without so much as a word. Hungry children eat anything you give them. An ounce of kindness. The most broken love. Even a crumb is enough when you are hungry. You take what is given and say *thank you*. When I finished I could see my skin glowing the way it once did, before Mother and I had to run. Styx, I noticed, was sitting on a small pile of skulls, watching me intently. Clearing my throat, I asked softly, 'Do you . . . do you know where my mother is?'

Styx Was Very Still

It was as though the river went quiet too.
For a second, nothing could be heard,
no rush of water on the rocks.

No haunting voices from beyond.
Not even the stir of the bats
over our heads.

'Hekate,' she spoke,
her voice barely above a whisper.
'The truth is, your mother . . . '

She hesitated.
My heart raced.
What happened to my mother?

Styx Looked into My Eyes

and for the first time
I saw kindness there,
but it was edged with sadness.
A devastating sort of paradox.

'I looked for her.
The truth is your mother . . .
she only had two choices
after she left you here.

She could either go with Zeus
or she could go with Poseidon.'
Styx reached for my shaking hand
and held it between her cold fingers.

Her next words were carefully chosen.
'Your mother did neither.'

My Mother's Choice

'Your mother is unlike any Goddess I know. It's why her gifts are so strange, they were crafted for a strange deity. We were girls together, her and I. Cousins, but more like sisters. And even then, when we were young – back when it was not dangerous for our family to be close – she was able to make the strangest things happen out of thin air. One day, she invented a fox made out of fire. None of us knew how she did it, only one night, she disappeared into the woods and came out with a creature bright as starfire, its swishing tail sparking embers across my father's river-flooded palace. We loved that fox. My sisters still love its descendants. Each of them has a cub and they cherish it like a child. She knew how to do this. Reach into us, find what was lacking and give us a sky full of something we did not realize we needed. So what Zeus and Poseidon wanted from her was not just herself, but all of her gifts. They did not understand that a Goddess like Asteria would find a way out of their quagmire, because Asteria was not a Goddess who could be possessed or owned through a trap. She was bright and shrewd, even when we were young. So when faced with this impossible choice, after she left you with us, she first became a hare, one of the fastest creatures in the world. But they became leopards and cornered her. Then, she became a bird. But they became eagles and nearly caught her. Which left her with her last and only choice. She flung herself into the sea. And she transformed herself into an island, full of birds and trees and a place where no God can go without her permission.'

Comfort Is a Peculiar Thing

No one teaches you how to find comfort
when all you have known is running, fear,
the collapsing walls of a once-palace,
where the only source of true stability
and love you have ever had is your mother.
And when she is ripped from you,
there is nothing anyone can tell you
that will bring you that strange emotion.
Comfort is for children who have not known war. Comfort is for
        children who have not been
left in dark places with strangers.
What Styx just told me gave me no comfort or joy.
All it told me was that my mother
was chased so far
that she finally ran out of land to run on.
The only place she had left was the ocean.
The only thing she could do as a Goddess, to get away from the
        cruelty of Gods, was turn herself into something
they would never want to possess.

An unwelcoming island in a stormy sea.

Styx Had Been Watching

I could see her looking at my features
with guarded caution,
trying to read my dark eyes,
wondering what I was debating
within my own mind.

I tilted my head slightly
and squeezed her hand in mine.
'If she is an island now,
can she turn back
when things are safe?'

Styx simply sighed,
her voice an ocean of pain.
She slowly shook her head
and spoke dreaded words I had
hoped would not leave her lips.

'No, little one.
Her bargain was
that she gave all her powers away
to become this island.
There is no way for her to return

to her divine body.
Not anymore.
This was the choice she made.
Not just for herself
but also to keep you safe.'

I Stilled

Everything around me felt thick
and heavy as though
I could not breathe and my heart was
about to stop. We were immortals.
How could this happen to one
of us? I felt myself falling to the
ground, tears unable to form, blurry
vision, throat tight like a thousand
different storms trying to break
through my skin. I wanted to crawl
outside of this hurricane-skin
that was holding me in.

'Are you saying,'
I whispered,

'that my mother
is *dead*?'

Death

Even here, in the kingdom of death itself, dying as an immortal felt like an impossibility. My only experience with death was the stories my mother gave me. She told me tales about how mortals are doomed, so everything is more beautiful to them yet more cruel because they live such short lives. She told me about the villages not far from us where once people died, their bodies would rot if not set aflame, but I had never seen decay until I saw the bones and skeletons of the Underworld. When a mortal died, prayers were given for their safe passage, a feast in their name. And yet, although my mother was a Goddess, a guide to stars and maker of prophecies, the creator of dreams, there was no one to attend her last rites, speak kindly of who she was. She left her immortal Goddess body to become an island, a death in every way that counted to the divine, completely alone.

Styx Put Her Arms Around Me

And I shuddered against her cold form.
She put her chin on my head,
spoke comfortingly to me.

'We do not die, child.
She is not dead,
not the way you are thinking.

Instead, you must picture her alive,
just in a different form.
Here, and not here.

We do not have to have
these bodies to continue
to exist.'

But it did not matter
how Styx saw it.
To me,

my mother,
my confidante,
my only friend,

was now truly *gone*.

'What Will I Do Now?'

I begged her to give me answers that a part of me knew she could not possibly have. But grief was a cruel, selfish thing. It wounded the one who carried it so deeply, that when others saw them, they only saw the wound. And that was all I was now. A wound. A motherless thing. A child grieving without even knowing what grief was. The question hung in the air. Styx simply held me in her cold arms, her wet hair against my body, but in my numbness I could not even feel the cold. She did not say a word; instead, just let me sob. For how was Styx to know how to comfort a child who had lost the only parent they had ever known? We sat like that for hours, her holding me close, this dreaded river that even the Gods were afraid of tenderly consoling a grieving child. Finally, when my tears had stopped from exhaustion, I heard her say, 'I promised your mother I would keep you safe, Hekate.'

From the Shadows, a Figure Spoke

'You cannot keep a God-child
from above here among
the corpses and cold, Styx.
She needs a home. A place to grow.'

This voice was unfamiliar
and it had the agedness of oceans.
When I squinted to look at the figure,
it looked like a mountain was moving.

I realized then that a giant was crouching
in the mouth of the entrance of this place.
His huge form began to slowly shrink
until he was the size of Charon.

'I know this, Pallas,' Styx snapped,
'What would you have me do precisely?
You know the river is my only home.
You have known this since we became consorts.'

Ah. So this was my uncle Pallas,
my father's only brother. My mother mentioned
his name just once, when reading
a message from my father.

The words had not made sense
to me then. But now,
in the cold light of afters,
everything was clearer.

'Pallas has betrayed us.
He has chosen the side

of the Olympians over us.
He has deceived your father.'

The knowledge of this betrayal
crystal-clear in my heart,
I glared at him. He was one
of the reasons my mother was gone.

He was why I never knew my father.
Pallas did not look at me,
or even notice my fierce glare.
Instead, he said to Styx,

'Four of our children
live in palaces on Olympus.
They are cared for in ways—'
Styx's voice rose to a screech.

'Do you think I do not know
how my children are being raised
in Zeus' kingdom?' Her eyes glowed
with molten amber fury.

Pallas raised his hands in surrender.
'You agreed to Zeus' gift, too.
It was an honour for our efforts
during the war.'

Through gritted teeth, Styx spoke.
'You know as well as I,
taking our children was
not a gift of any kind.
What Zeus was trying to prevent
was our children growing up
with any ideas of Titan rebellion.'
My eyes widened at these words.

Of course. Of course, that was why
Styx's children had been taken.
The war may be over now,
but the threat of the Titans rebelling

was a good enough reason for Zeus
to divide us, imprison us,
separate us, even under the guise
of magnanimous 'gifts'.

Pallas chose his next words carefully.
'Even so, we now have a Titan child left.
So let me do what I can, and build her
a home on your riverbanks.'

How to Build a Home for a Godling

First you must choose a place where a child feels safe. And this is difficult. For some children do not know what safety looks like. They must be taught. So you let them choose the ground, and in this case, it is the ground far enough from the mossy, rock-covered riverbanks that she cannot hear the spirits, but close enough that the River Goddess can come and go as she pleases. Second, when you begin to build, let her help you. She may be suspicious of you, for you betrayed everyone she loved, but she is a child looking for something to do. Let her see how you raise pristine white marble from the palm of your hand and turn the work of a thousand mortals into a job for simply two Gods. Which brings us to the third. You let her only friend help, in this case the ferryman who once in a while takes leave from his duties serving the dead and the River Goddess to comfort a forgotten child. Perhaps because long ago he was a forgotten child too. Fourth, when you finish building this home, a palace just for a Goddess' child, you give her one final gift. Inside her chambers, make her a secret window made of adamantine and sacred glass to look into the world above. Let her have one place within this darkness where the sunshine comes through.

Pallas

used to be a God of Warcraft.
But Zeus could not allow this,
so he took some of his gifts
to maintain control over him.

Then Pallas became a God of Craftmanship.
He built palaces and weapons.
I did not often see much of him
as he was always wandering the earth.

His gifts of creation were
always needed in the land of the living.
But his real love was crafting
wooden toys. His daughter Bia,

he told me once, loved wooden toys. When
he visited, he filled my palace with his small gifts.
Once, I asked him about his brother, my father,
but his eyes darkened with something

unnamed and he stormed out of my halls.
The next day I found a carefully crafted
eagle sitting over the fireplace.
A gift, an explanation or an apology?

Perhaps all three.

The Grief Abated as I Grew Older

But something else took its place:
a wish, a curiosity, call it a thirst.
It came from the knowledge left to me
by Charon.

All things have a purpose.
Not every purpose is good.

In my palace, all alone,
the more I thought about this,
the more my need grew to know
what he meant.

Time passed so slowly for immortals,
but it did pass. In Styx's waters
I saw my body was growing,
my childhood escaping from me.

I was a lonely child.
Lonely in ways I had never been
inside my mother's home.
I felt her absence sharply.

Like an eagle's talon lodged
inside my heart, a constant wound.
Perhaps my curiosity
is what I used to fill the hole it left.

All things have a purpose.
Not every purpose is good.

Charon

Our friendship happened slowly.
One day he brought me food
and the next, he brought me a story.
And when I enjoyed the tale,
he told me another.
His work in the Underworld
was to transport recently dead
spirits to the realm in which they would
spend eternity.
They brought with them his payment
in two coins, placed on their corpses
before they were cremated.
Apparently, he took the coins
as means of tradition,
but what he valued most
from those he ferried were the tales
they had collected over their lives.
Soon, this became a habit.
He would visit me in my new home
and find me by my sunlit window.
Together, we would take in
a sunrise or a sunset.
And he would tell me one
of the many stories he received
from his many passengers.

A Conversation with Charon

We were sitting at the window again,
playing a game of dice,
when I asked him about his parents.
'What was your father like?'

He paused the game and frowned.
'My father is Erebus, the darkness.
I have only met him a few times
in my mother's palace. She raised me.'

It's odd how much is revealed
about a parent from three lines.
Most of us were fathered by Gods
we did not know well at all.

'And your mother?' I asked quietly,
picking up the dice to restart the game.
He looked down contemplatively,
then steepled his fingers.

'Nyx is the Night itself,'
he said finally. His voice sounded
strange and strangled.
'She is powerful. So powerful

that even those new Gods on
Olympus are fearful of her.'
This caught my attention
and I looked at his face sharply.

But he wasn't looking at me.
He was focused on the game.

'Growing up in the Realm of Night
is less growth, more survival.

My brothers and sisters and I,
you can say we had an interesting
upbringing, and that is why
we are interesting Gods.'

I was perplexed. 'Are you certain
you are not a God of Oracles?'
His bushy eyebrows furrowed.
'What makes you say that?'

I triumphantly tossed down
a perfect hand as I answered,
'You speak in riddles better
than most of my mother's Oracles did.'

Charon's face cleared
and he threw his head back,
his deep laughter echoing across
the halls of my palace.

Lessons in Cartography

It was hard to know how many mortal years I had spent in Hades already. The task of time was meant for those doomed to death, and there seemed little need for me to count my days in any similar way. So instead, I became a collector of stories to learn more about my new home. I asked Styx how far her waters flowed and she told me that she was one of five rivers here. Charon told me about Acheron, the river where he ferried the dead. When I wouldn't stop begging Pallas, he would pause his carving and tell me about the other parts of Hades: the Elysian Fields, the Vale of Mourning and the Halls of the Night. I stored all of this away inside my mind until I could craft a careful map. With ink upon parchment I slowly drew every single story Styx, Charon and Pallas gave me.

But What Lay Beyond These Riverbanks?

I found myself lying awake with this question often. Gods did not need sleep, but we did sleep for pleasure. However I tossed and turned, picturing the stories about this dark realm which was now my home. I *had* to know more. It was like a hand wrapping around my throat, this curiosity. It would not let me *breathe*.

One day, the need was so strong I made my plan. I told no one. Not Styx when she visited. Not Charon when he came to sit with me by my window. Not Pallas on his rare trips to my palace with a new carved gift. I waited until all was quiet before I moved through those heavy doors onto the familiar riverbanks. Here, I was even more caught in the feeling of emptiness when I saw the endless darkness around the glowing river.

No wonder I felt compelled towards the water: it was the only source of real light around, even if it was coming from the infinite souls occupying its depths. Was this the only place the dead lived? I had asked Charon, and he had hesitated before saying no. There was more to this place. But no matter how much I begged, he would not elaborate. So I went where I had seen his boat go. I walked along the riverbanks to see where the river led. I was strong now, nourished from regular meals of ambrosia and nectar.

Strength does not mean invincibility, Styx had once warned me when she found me trying to reach for the waters again. As I walked, my heart pounding and a feeling of adventure in my bones, I realized that strength is the capacity for so much more than invincibility.

It fed the need and hunger for *more*.

Finally a Light

It was small at first.
The darkness of this place
nearly swallowed up the glow
from my small lamp,
but I could see in the distance
a crack of light.
It was long and thin,
and the closer I got,
the bigger it got.
My feet quickened their pace
and my heartbeat felt like a drum.
As I approached faster and faster,
I heard a voice from the distance.
It was familiar . . .

Hekate

It sounded like my mother.
I wanted to run to her,
but there was only so fast
my legs could carry me.

Hekate

And then I realized
where that beam of light
was coming from.
It was the opening
between a pair of
massive granite doors.

But

before I could reach it
I heard something shift
close to me.

A soft rattle of a chain.
A sound of shuffling.
A snort, and then a low, soft growl.

As I turned my head,
I was met with six glowing red eyes
and the collective roar of three huge heads.

Thump, Thump, Thump

The sound of my heart
battering my rib cage.

Thump, thump, thump

The creature edged closer
and I slowly stepped back.

Thump, thump, thump

The light was right behind it,
making it a massive, ominous silhouette.

Thump, thump, thump

I scrambled backwards
as it started gaining on me.

Thump, thump, thump

A howl escaping its throat,
It lunged at me and I fell back—

'Cerberus!'

A commanding voice filled
every edge of the darkness.

The dog-monster stopped so suddenly
that even I halted.

'Stop.
Not her!'

I heard it whine softly
like it was a much smaller pup

and not the monstrous,
three-headed thing it was.

Then, to my surprise,
it lay down and thumped its huge tail

and I heard the words,
'Good dog.'

Hades and Cerberus

Have you ever heard the story of the boy who was left to his own devices? A boy with a loud family always at war with each other? A boy who simply wanted peace and quiet and could not find it in the confines of a mountain populated with Gods? And what does a boy like that, who does not like his own kind, do for company? On one of his walks away from the mountain, he passes through a village. And he finds a little puppy abandoned on the street. Very much like him, the dog does not fit in. It has three heads and, fearing it is cursed by the Gods, no one wants it. So the boy picks up the puppy. Holds it close to his chest. All three of the puppy's heads whine and nestle closer to him. He wraps the dog inside his clothes and brings it to his mountain home to raise it as his own. Calls it Cerberus and blesses it with immortality, and, like any good story which involves two beings finding family and understanding in each other, the two became inseparable. And now the boy was the king of the Underworld and the dog, who always loved his boy more than anything in the world, guarded his home.

Meeting Cerberus

At the end of the day
even the biggest of dogs
are just that.

Dogs.

And watching this massive beast
suddenly turn into
the most docile

and friendly of giants
was enough
to melt any heart.

Mine was no exception.

A Difference

Hades, his hand on Cerberus' middle head,
smiled at his monster dog,
then turned to me and his smile faded.

'You should not be here.'
I could tell he was trying to be harsh with me,
his tone strict,

but I suppose it was difficult
when the big dog rolled over submissively,
his behaviour puppy-like.

Hades glared at me and said,
'I think it's time for you to go back home.'
I swallowed hard and turned

and in that moment
Cerberus whined again
and I heard, 'Hekate, wait.'

I realized as I looked at him,
this boy-God-King,
whatever he was in these realms,

that at one point in his life
he had been just a Godling like me.
Before he was King of the Underworld

he used to be just like me.
And perhaps he too recognized
loneliness well.

'Why Did You Come Here?'

His question was quiet
but I could feel the curiosity
and the fire behind it.

I folded my arms around myself.
A sudden feeling of cold
was inside my very bones.

'I thought I heard my mother.'
I said this quietly,
'Behind those doors.'

He turned and looked at the doors,
the pool of soft light
that flowed from them.

When he looked back at me
his dark-bright eyes were softer,
and he spoke more gently.

'That is the world of the dead.
Your mother is not there.
She is an island in a stormy sea.'

'What of My Father?'

When the messenger had flown
into our disintegrating palace,
he had only told us all was lost.
No one told us what had happened

to my Titan father after the Olympians
had won control in the Titanomachy.
I had thought about him often,
a God who made me, but I had never met.

The question of him always troubled me.
It visited me in my dreams sometimes.
You see, immortals cannot be killed.
So what happens to them after a war?

What happens to Gods who are defeated
but are cursed to remain alive after?
A grimace crossed Hades' face
and the hand at his side tightened into a fist.
'He is here. In the Underworld.'

'My Father Is Here?'

Maybe the voice calling me was his?
Maybe that was why the light called to me?
Despite it all, I was a hopeful child.
Despite it all, I needed my father.

My heart clung to this idea tightly,
that the voice calling to me
was the voice of my father,
praying for help from the Underworld.

'Please. You must let me go to him.'
There was a soft sorrow in Hades' eyes
when he looked into mine.
But within a fleeting second it was gone.

And then he drew himself up
to his full proud height
as ruler of this realm and said,
'No. I cannot allow that.'

'Has This Place Made You So Cold, Oh King?'

Styx's voice rose from the waters,
and when I turned I saw her lift herself
from the river, like a siren from the sea.

I wanted to apologize to her for straying,
I wanted to run to her and embrace her tightly,
even though I knew she would hate it.

Instead, I stood still and let her walk to me.
When she did, she took my hand
in her cold wet fingers and held it gently.

'You should have stayed home, Hekate,'
she said, but the words were not angry.
They were deeply sad.

I looked at her and then at Hades.
A sudden wave of fear gripped me.
'What is it,' I asked softly,

'that you are not telling me?'

Secrets

I did not realize it until that moment: Styx's avoidance of me, her brief visits only to ensure the essentials of feeding me ambrosia and nectar, was for reasons other than her river of oaths and death keeping her so preoccupied. Hades making a promise to my mother regarding my safety and then disappearing was not just because he was otherwise engaged ruling the Underworld. They were both hiding something from me. My mother hid things from me too. She would not name who was chasing us until the very end, even though I knew it was two powerful Gods. Everyone assumed that to protect children, they must be kept in the dark – no one understood those secrets haunted the same children they were so ardently trying to protect. I was beginning to recognize that eternity was a very long time and if this was now my home, I would not abide any more secrets. Not from those who were meant to take care of me. So I took my hand back from Styx and told her and Hades, 'If I am to live here, I want to know everything. Every secret. Every wound. Every truth.'

Styx Exchanged a Look with Hades

and then he slowly nodded at her.
She took my hand again and said,

'Hold on tight,
and whatever happens,
whoever calls you,
no matter what you see,
Hekate, do *not* let go.'

An Entrance

We were still standing by Cerberus
and those heavy stone doors
just ajar with beguiling light
slipping through the crack.

Hades touched one of the doors
with his large, pale hand
and it glowed red
where he touched it.

Slowly the spill of light
filled the caves and
I was gazing into
blinding brightness

so sharp I had to cover my eyes.
But I felt Styx's hand gently tug
on mine, and my feet moved
forward into the white abyss.

First, It Was the Asphodel Meadows

Slowly the brightness gave way to a haze of mists flowing over lavender fields. This was no longer the cave or the riverbanks I had come to know so well – it was wide and open. I almost forgot where I was until I looked up and saw that it was still the underbelly of the earth, tree roots hanging down over the dome. This place was not cold like the cave, but nor was it hot like the garden in the palace I grew up in. My mother once told me about this place. Like mortals hear stories about Gods, we are told stories about them. In her story there was a man who led a life that was neither good nor evil. She said he lived a largely insignificant life. This was where souls like his were sent. Most mortals after death ended up here, in these lavender fields where nothing ever truly happened. I saw souls wander about lost. 'What are they doing?' I whispered to Styx as Hades guided us wordlessly. I noticed that the spirits were careful to keep away from him but they looked at us with curiosity. Styx glanced down at me as I grasped her hand tighter. Her lips lifted slightly, in what I presumed was reassurance, and her fangs glinted in the soft grey light. 'They are waiting.' I looked back at them as they wandered across these seemingly infinite fields. 'What are they waiting for?' Styx shook her head. 'That is what this place is. Infinite waiting.'

Fields' End

To my child's eyes, Asphodel
looked infinite, the fields
leading into an endless horizon.

But Styx, Hades and I
were immortals and we walked
the way Gods walked, never tiring,

quick in step and able to cover
more distance than mortal bodies
could ever walk or run.

To my surprise, the fields did end
and the ground returned to cool
polished dark stones making a path

that led to a bridge in the distance.
Before I could think more
on the fog that surrounded it,

or the strange light that rose
from beneath the bridge,
I heard a cold, awful wailing.

Kokytos

It was a sound so full of despair,
so profoundly mournful
that I wanted to cover my ears.

What could make such a noise?
I squinted my eyes to see another river,
this one cut between a smooth floor.

So perfectly shaped,
I almost didn't think of it
as a river at all.

All around it walked spirits,
translucent, barely there,
threads of mourning connecting them.

Every now and then
they would stop to drink
from the waters of this river,

and as they lifted their heads
they would wail and mourn,
all over again.

'This is Kokytos,' Styx whispered,
'The river of lamentation.
Every soul who drinks these waters

feels a mourning so deep they cry out.
But the river's water is addictive
and they cannot stop drinking it.'

I Shuddered

What a cruel way to spend eternity.
Sending yourself into suffering
over and over again,
without recognizing the damage.

'But why do they do this?'
I asked Styx, shivering
as a translucent soul walked
all the way through me.

Styx put her hand forward
and the souls around us
disappeared as we crossed
the bridge together.

'They spent a life causing others
misery and because misery
is all their soul remembers,
despair is where they return.'

'Styx,' I said softly
as we reached Hades on the other side,
'does nectar not do the same thing
to us and our bodies?'

I remember my mother and I
starving, sick, bare-boned
and scarcely able to ensure
our immortal bodies kept moving.

Styx looked down at me,
her expression unreadable.

She shook her head,
but her eyes held

a different answer.

The Ground

was slowly becoming warmer and warmer.
I looked down at my feet as we walked
and saw the smoke begin to rise,
orange streams of fire flowed between
the grooves of polished stone.

I did not know where we were going,
I did not know what was coming up.
I swallowed hard as grey light
turned into orange and yellow,
and my skin became hot.

I could see the dark primordial
mountains looming before us.
A cold shudder ran through
my still-growing body.
I wanted to turn and run.

But my mother had told me
to have courage
and so I kept walking,
clutching hard at
Styx's hand.

Hades Led Us Quietly

It was easy to forget
that we were following him.
His footsteps were so soft.

I had learned his story
from my mother years ago,
when we were still at war.
Hades was the youngest
of the three Olympian brothers,
children of the once-ruling Titans,

Rhea, the mother Goddess,
and Kronos, God of Time
and God-King of the world.

But Kronos had a madness,
a sickness no one could cure.
His father had cursed him

and told him that someday
one of his own children
would steal his throne.

To prevent this from happening,
Kronos ate every one
of his five offspring.

Rhea, pregnant with her sixth
and consumed with grief,
found a way to protect her child.

Zeus grew up in secret
and returned to defeat Kronos,

releasing his sisters and brothers
from the stomach-prison of the old God.
They arrived in reverse order
of their original births.

First it was Hera, then Poseidon,
then Demeter, Hades and finally,
Hestia. After which the three brothers

looked upon the realms of the sky,
the sea and the Underworld
and chose which one to rule.

But to be ruler of the Underworld
you must choose never to live
on Olympus with the other Gods.

A Realization

'Hades chose to live here?'
I asked Styx, in confusion.
It was a realm more difficult
than skies or sea could ever be.

'He did not want Olympus,'
Styx told me softly,
'and he wanted nothing
to do with his brothers after the war.'

I looked at Styx now,
but she was staring
at the frame of the young God
as he walked surefooted ahead.

'Did he fight?' I asked.
She turned to me sharply now.
'Hekate, not all of us had a choice. Hades had to
fight. But he regretted it deeply.

I remember his feet soaked in
the golden blood of all his loved ones.
I think it was then he decided
to work only with the dead.'

I stared at the shape before us,
silently making his way into the inferno.
He was so unafraid,
but there was an ancient sadness there.

Something told me clearly
that the Titanomachy stole from Hades,
just like it had stolen
something irreplaceable from me.

A Roar Exploded Too Close

The sound was so violent
that the stone under my feet vibrated.
I clung to Styx's hand
out of fear
but also out of awe.
What could possibly
have made such a sound?

The Sounds Grew Louder

A howl.
Hooves.
The flight of something
far too big to be a bird.

And still we walked towards it.
'We can go back,'
Styx whispered to me.
But I shook my head.

As we kept walking
I saw it.
A waterfall of flames,
the bright orange strange

against the abyss of black
we had been walking through.
For a second
I thought we would jump,

but instead, Hades
took us right to the edge
and stopped.
Below us, the hot bright liquid

glittered like the sun.
And sputtered like death.

'Tartarus'

Hades' voice was a whisper,
but it was not because he was scared.
It was because he was reverent.

It was strange that this boy-God
still found a reason to be reverent
towards a place within his domain.

And yet, as he whispered,
a door opened within the waterfall,
an impossible door

in an impossible place.
The more I saw of this realm,
the more it terrified me.

What was Tartarus?
I wondered as I heard the sounds
just beyond the door.

I swallowed hard
and considered quietly
whether coming here

was a wise idea at all.

Hades Went First

And for a second,
it looked like he had disappeared
into an abyss of darkness.

But then he extended his hand
and I hesitated before taking it.
Because somewhere deep inside

I knew whatever I saw beyond
this door would change me forever.
But I was a child of war.

My childhood was made
of endings and running
and losing so much already.

I raised my head high,
kept hold of Styx's hand
and the chasm swallowed me

whole.

The Fall

I felt myself falling,
and the ground beneath me
was nowhere to be found.

My arms and legs flailed
as I braced myself to
meet the ground

whipping through the air
as my lungs let out a scream
so loud, so long.

But still
I did not meet
the ground.

And then
I realized
something terrifying.

Within the fall,
I had somehow lost
Styx's hand.

'Hekate!'

I heard a familiar voice
shout my name across
the blinding darkness.

I was still falling,
it felt like it had been
years and years of this.

And still I heard my name,
as though the person calling me
were so close by.

Finally, a hand
grasped mine
and I was about to claw it

because I did not know
who it was
or *what* it was.

But suddenly,
it was like
a thousand stars burst alive

and the darkness
was chased out
by the light.

I Hit the Ground

I fell upon it
on my front

and banged my head,
every part of me aching.

But Styx's hand dragged me
back to my feet

and she studied my head, frowning.
'You're bleeding.'

Hades appeared behind her
and tore a bit of his robe,

then handed it to Styx's waiting hand.
I touched my forehead

and my fingers came away with gold.
I tried to be brave and not make a sound.

But my vision swam
as I looked around.

It was a chamber of white,
like a blank canvas.

Styx pressed the fabric against my head
and I hissed in pain.

'It's a surface wound, Hekate,'
she said impatiently.

'I did tell you,
not to let go of my hand.'

Suddenly the Chamber Dissolved

And all around me I saw fire,
fire everywhere,

fire that licked at us
and yet did not burn us.

Hades looked at my confused face
and said,

'It cannot harm us.
It only harms those that live here.'

I felt a chill despite the heat.
What could possibly live here?

This Crumbling, Burning World

My mother once told me about a place.
A place feared by mortals and immortals alike.

In her stories, she spoke of rivers of fire,
of ground that was hot, glowing coals.

She called this a realm of torment
but before I could ask her more,

she changed the subject.
What I saw here was so much worse,

a place beyond imagination.
All around me I heard the roars,

and it struck me like a slap to the face.
Those roars were not of anger.

They were wails of pain, a hunger for freedom.
An eternity of beings all trapped

in a burning forever.

'Why Are We Here?'

I asked Styx softly.
She would not look at me.
Hades did.

His pale skin reflected
the red and yellow
of the flames,

As he said quietly,
'This is where he is.
Your father.'

Devastation

Has someone ever
changed your existence
with just a few words?

Has the world
beneath your feet
ever simply fallen away?

I thought I knew terror.
I thought I had faced loss.
But nothing could prepare me

for this.
For just a few seconds
I too was Atlas,

all of the heavens
on my shoulders
crushing me

till nothing was left.

'Do You Still Want to See Him?'

It was the way Styx asked this question.
She was not one to speak so quietly.
Whispers were not a familiar sound from her.

Neither was fear.
But when I saw her face,
I saw it. She was afraid.

Of what? What was I about to see?
I looked at her, then at Hades.
A steely determination gripped me.

'Yes.'

A Walk Through Tartarus

I knew I had to be brave.
It was what my mother taught me.
Courage would be the name of my story.

So with Hades leading us
and Styx holding my hand tight,
we crossed the river of fire.

Stepping on raised stone
after raised stone,
it felt like the river

stretched on forever.
And then, finally we were there.
On the other side.

And there it was,
a mountain made of flames.
So tall that you could not see the top.

Hades reached into it.
And with a scraping sound
he opened a door made of fire.

And we stepped into
A pool of ichor.

A Secret

Do you know what happens
to Gods after they lose a war?

Their wives and daughters are stolen.
But the male Gods, their fate

is something far more hideous.
Atlas was fortunate.

They only gave him the burden
of the whole wide world.

But my father and the other
Titans who stood against the Olympians

were not so lucky.
You see,

the floors of Olympus
were meant to be gold.

Gold the colour of regency.
Gold the colour of nobility.

Gold. The colour of Gods' blood.

My Father

I had never met him,
but I knew him from
the shape of his face and nose.

They were just like mine.
I resembled him
more than my mother.

Now he was nothing but a body
among hundreds of other
gigantic bodies.

He was drawn up against
the inner wall of the cavern
held by thick, adamantine chains.

His blood flowed into
the veins of the mountain,
and turned the whole of it

into the colour of ichor.
No one ever asked
what made the mountain
shine like it was gold.

No one dared.
Because no one
really wanted to know.

In Horror, My Mind Pieced the Aftermath Together

So this was how a God was destroyed.
This was how they ensured Titans
would never rise up again against
these brand-new Gods.

I felt my knees weaken,
the brutality of the truth
almost too much for my small body
to handle.

It wasn't enough to defeat us.
They had to take every God
who stood up against them
and drain them of their blood.

Blood they built palaces on,
rejoiced on and ruled from
in their beautiful Olympus.
How did they forget,

when they walked upon
those golden floors every day,
that the surface they walked on,
the gold of their beautiful mountain,

came from the blood of those
they once called *family*?

Styx Let Go of My Hand

I did not notice because I was so fixated.
This army of drained Gods
were my uncles and cousins.

But at the time, I could only think of my father.
My father. Tortured. Alone.
Here for eternity.

'Please. Can you not release him?'
I begged.
Hades' expression was unreadable.

'I cannot, Hekate. This is his destiny.
This is your only chance to see him.
I suggest you use it well.'

I Wanted to Be Angry

If I was older, if I had any power,
I would unleash it all
to rescue my parents.

But I had nothing.
No one had told me
what sort of Goddess I was.

The poniard of longing
pierced my soul again.
When would I harness my power?

So instead,
I walked to where my father was chained,
feet slipping in slick gold.

My hands balled into
fists by my side,
nails digging into my skin.

Slowly, I reached out,
my hand shaking,
and I touched his knee.

A Giant Eye Opened

A roar escaped his lips,
as though disturbed from deep
and cold slumber.

Then his eyes fell on me
and my very bones shuddered.
There was so much anguish in his face.

So much rage and torment.
I opened my mouth to speak.
At first nothing came out.

Finally I said the word.
The word I had never ever said to him aloud.
'Father?'

First His Anger Filled the Room

It was like waking the sun in the middle of the night, the fury and the rage of it. At the sound of the word from my lips, he stopped. His eyes looked into mine, as though trying to recognize me. He was colossal, so much bigger than me. If he wanted, he could crush me between his fingers and be done with it. Instead, amber tears started to fall down his face. His arms reached out to me, but the shackles held him back. 'Hekate?' I nodded vigorously to tell him, *yes, yes it is me*. His tears flowed freely now as he wearily beckoned me to come closer. 'I am sorry I have not been able to fulfil my duties to you as your father. But there is one gift I can give you. A gift no other God-child has ever had. I apologize that I only have one gift for you, my daughter, when you deserve a hundred, a thousand more. But this is all I have to give you.' My heart broke as I watched him pull at the unforgiving shackles until suddenly . . . I felt the ground move under my feet and I was raised up to him. I turned and saw Hades, his hand aloft as though holding the ground up till my father could rest his large hand on my head. I turned back as my father began to speak. 'My dearest daughter. I prophesize that you will be the Goddess of the strangest things. I prophesize the dead will bow to you as you move in their wake. And most of all, I prophesize that you will be free, in a way I will never ever be.'

'Hekate. It's Time to Go'

When I heard Styx's voice calling to me,
I did not turn around.

'I'm not leaving you,'
I said to him, my hands balled in fists of rage.

My father smiled at me,
'You cannot help me, child.'

It felt like a blow to my chest,
like my heart itself was crushed.

'Please, there has to be a way.'
I looked desperately around him,

but all I saw were other tired immortals
who had given up just like him.

'Dear one.' He touched my cheek
and I felt the slick ichor left on my skin.

'This is my fate now.
Among my brothers.

I am no coward.
I will not run from this.

I, too, would not have been kind
to the Olympians had they lost.'

There was a coldness to these words
that sent a shiver through me.

'Still,' I pleaded, 'No one deserves
an eternity of this.'

But he was already gone,
far away in his pain-filled dream,

his eyes in a distant place.
I took a deep, shaky breath,

and with blood-soaked feet,
felt myself returned to the floor.

I backed away from my father,
feeling sick with anguish.

Styx took my hand as I reached her and Hades.
We were silent on the journey back.

I promise, I whispered to myself,
One day, I will free him.

I will free them all.

On Reflection

My parents were both Gods.
My father, Perses, was the Titan God of War.
My mother, Asteria, was the Titanide
of Oracles and Shooting Stars.

They once owned a palace
so grand that every God
and demi-God talked of it
with such great awe.

And my birth was supposed
to be a joyous occasion.
But this was before the war.
And now my parents,

once a God and a Goddess,
served the rest of their eternities
as an island in the middle of nowhere
and a slave in the worst realm

of all the mortal and immortal worlds.

A DANGEROUS
GIRLHOOD

PART TWO

Girlhood

It happened so fast that I almost did not notice it. When a child is raised between bones and ghosts, they learn about death faster than they learn about growing up. I was too focused on my dreams of rescuing my parents. So when the ichor in my body swelled and turned me from child to girl, I did not even recognize it until one day, staring at myself in a mirror made of the River Acheron that Charon had gifted me, I saw it. The lengthening of my legs and my arms. My widening hips. The discomfort of an almost-woman body. Where were my full cheeks? Even my hair had lengthened to my waist and I had to keep it braided so it was no longer in my way. Now, when I looked into my eyes, I saw the violet shades of my mother's. In fact, I was starting to resemble her more and more as time went on, but the more I resembled her, the shifting sands of time took my father from my features. Is that all ageing is? Leaving things you knew and once loved behind to become something brand new?

Styx Visited More Often Now

The halls of my palace on her riverbanks
were no longer as empty as they once were.

Since that day in Tartarus,
something had changed.

Ever since then, Styx took her evening
nectar and ambrosia with me.

She would ask me about my day,
and tell me about the souls she ate.

This used to scare me, but I understood
the rules of godhood better now.

I still did not know my gifts precisely.
But one day I walked

to the mouth of the cave the river
came through and found violet flowers.

I put them inside a pot in the kitchen
and carefully stole a thimbleful of Styx's water.

When I added it to the flowers,
I watched as they turned a vibrant blue,

then a violent yellow and then the whole pot
melted into a mess of yellow metal.

And my halls smelled for days
of a strange fragrance I could not name.

If Styx noticed, she did not say anything.
But Pallas, my uncle, on one of his visits

commented upon it. 'Have you been burning
Krokos in here? I keep smelling saffron.'

Krokos. That was the name of the first
of many, many flowers I would one day know.

It was also the first time this dark palace
began to feel familiar, like the home

I had once known.

Attempts at Discovery

Styx, Pallas and Charon
all tried to help me
discover my powers.

Styx brought me to
a lake of tears in the Underworld
and showed me how to control water.

I tried for days and the water
would not rise to my fingers.
Pallas showed me fire,

and how to forge.
But I simply made a mess
of every metal I tried to tame.

Charon showed me
how to manipulate the winds.
But try as I might,

I could not create
even a slight breeze
to take me anywhere.

I was determined
to find out
what I could be.

But no matter what I did,
the discovery of who I was meant
to be felt out of reach.

A Strange Meeting

As a child I ached for company,
but now that I was older,
I yearned for it even more.

I wanted to talk to someone
who knew their purpose,
someone perhaps my own age.

When the yearning grew too loud
and during the days that Charon,
Pallas and Styx were nowhere to be seen,

I would walk with my lantern
to a safe distance
from where Cerberus stood.

He growled and barked
but the noise of another being
that breathed in this place where

nothing seemed to breathe
gave the restlessness in me
a little bit of peace.

I would sit for hours,
until he got tired of his barking
and lay down, one pair of six eyes

watching me suspiciously.
It happened on a day like this.
I was sitting with my lantern,

Cerberus straining against his chain,
all three heads barking at me,
when a voice spoke to me from the dark.

'If you want to be friends with him
you need to give him treats.'
I frowned, turning my light

in the direction of the voice.
That was when I saw him.
A boy with shorn hair

and an angular face, dressed
in long robes. But it was his eyes that sang.
They were so tired and yet so kind.

He held a staff in one hand
and in his other hand,
three red, red cuts of raw meat.

Unlike his reaction with me
Cerberus whined in the direction
of this visitor, his huge tail thumping.

The boy stepped forward
and gently placed the meat
before each head.

The three-headed dog
devoured them hungrily.
And then the boy reached forward

and touched one of Cerberus' heads.
'Hello, little one,' he whispered,
'It has been some time.'

'Little one?' I exclaimed,
'He is three times the size of a lion!'
The boy chuckled at this.

'All dogs are little ones to me.
I see them all from birth to death.'
He looked at me.

'Would you like to try being friends
with him now? He should be docile.'
I nodded and stood up.

The dog's closest head turned to me
and a soft growl escaped his throat.
But when I showed him my hand,

he snuffled it softly
and, swallowing hard,
I reached out and touched his nose.

Cerberus whined and thumped
his tail even harder.
And I smiled. 'So this is how

we become friends.
I shall remember the treats
from now on.'

I turned to thank the boy
but to my surprise, he was gone.

Styx's Rules for Me

1. Do not leave the caves.
2. Do not go near my river.
3. Do not TOUCH my river's waters.
4. I mean it, Hekate, *do not* touch my river's waters – I will know.
5. Do not talk to spirits.
6. Definitely do not make friends with spirits.
7. Do not play with Cerberus, his duty is protecting the gates.
8. Do not steal my wine.
9. Do not walk through the doors to the Underworld without my permission or permission from Hades.
10. Do not speak to any Gods or Goddesses who you do not know.

I Broke (Most of) the Rules

Mostly because I was bored
but, as Styx and Pallas said,
I was headstrong.

The first rule I broke
was the one about leaving
the caves. Outside,

there was a forest full of irises
and violets and roses.
I did not travel far

from the mouth of the cave,
but I did collect herbs
to crush under my mortar

and pestle to see what happened,
combining them with ambrosia
or nectar to eat and drink.

Once I turned my feet turquoise
by drinking a concoction of herbs,
and Styx had to help turn them back

to the colour they naturally were.
I took meat to Cerberus,
which my kitchen provided,

for it was blessed with the ability
to provide anything I ever needed,
each pot filled with what I desired.

I played with Cerberus all the time.
I carefully used Styx's waters
in my strange flower potions.

I stole Styx's wine
and even shared some
with Charon when he came by

to play dice
or tell me stories.
And still, I wanted *more*.

There is only so long an immortal child
can be left to her own devices.
My mother once told me that as a child

she had countless cousins to play with.
Naiads and Oceanids, water nymphs
and River Gods. But I had no playmates.

Pallas had taught me how to carve
horses and bears and wolves
out of the bones left of mortals

who had ventured too far
and ended up drinking Styx's water.
But carving was a poor replacement

for a playmate. So I decided
one day long ago to walk
through those forbidden doors.

Not only would I talk to ghosts,
but perhaps ghosts would make
good companions.

The Fields of Asphodel

had become my favourite place to visit.
I knew that the mist felt dull to some,
but to me, it was mysterious.

I knew that the lavender in the fields
only added to the grey of the mist,
but flowers signalled a form of life.

Perhaps I was simply fascinated
by the waiting people
who walked into this place.

They would awaken confused here.
Sometimes they would stop to ask me
where they were, and tell me their story.

Like the woman who was once queen
until her husband and his lover poisoned her,
but she had died leaving a curse over them.

Or the man who escaped wolves
by singing them to slumber
only to step on a sleeping adder.

Death truly was a great equalizer.
For where else could you find a king
and a fisherman playing cards together?

Asphodel taught me that the Gods
may be eternal but mortals
have the very best of stories.

Tales From the Mortal World

I would sit in awe and listen
to ghosts tell the tales
of their lives.

They spoke of sickness but
also of joy.
Fear but also of tenderness.

I once met a man
who travelled the high seas
and fell in love with a siren.

He spoke of the ocean
with such love even though
its waters were what killed him.

But the most heartbreaking stories
came from children
taken long before their time.

One small child told me
that all he got was two thousand
sunrises before he lost his breath.

So this was how they measured
their lives, in the span of sunrises
and moonsets.

There were tales of parents
who lost their children,
and lovers who lost each other.

But a thread ran through all,
and that thread was named love.
When asked if they would

ever want to live again
they all said they would
if only to know love once more.

The Asphodel Fields
and their eternity of spirits
were my education on mortals
but most of all
on love.

War Seen Through Different Eyes

War is different
for those who are finite.
I learned this from
the stories mortals told me.

Immortals lived past it
yet mortals saw war as an ending.
To us in the Underworld,
every ending was a beginning.

If you were fortunate enough,
you awoke in the verdant green
of the glowing Elysian Fields,
a place where the virtuous and heroic went.

But most mortals at the end of a war
came to the Asphodel Meadows.
War brought a great influx of lost souls.
I watched them, hidden away in the mists.

The last time there was a war on Earth,
I tried to count how many dead
awakened in the mists of these
quiet, grey meadows.

I learned quickly never to do that again.

Duty

When Styx first caught me
all by myself in Asphodel
she had been deeply upset
and did not hide her displeasure.

'It is not your duty to be there,'
she said, gripping my arm
and nearly dragging me back
to my palace.

'Why!' I had cried out,
shocked by her forcefulness,
and she turned to me,
her split eyes cold with fury.

'Hekate, I made a promise
to your mother to keep you safe.
The only immortals who roam
the Underworld do so

out of duty to Hades or
because they have been
imprisoned by another God,
but never ever by choice.'

When we arrived at the palace,
she let go of my arm
and I rubbed it where
she had gripped me,

a frown forming on my face.
'I too am not here by choice,'

I told her sullenly. 'I should
be allowed to roam too.'

The anger in her features softened,
'You are a child of war,
and the Underworld is no place
for children, God or mortal.'

She added quietly,
'There are beings here
that even Hades cannot control.
Beings that could harm you.'

A chill ran down my spine
at her words. 'What kind of beings?'
But she ignored my question and
simply touched my face.

'Just know that staying
in this palace is the only way
I can keep you safe.
This realm alone is my domain.

You can only go into
the Asphodel Meadows
if they become a part
of your duties.'

A Pull

I tried to occupy myself
within the palace to appease
Styx. One of the clay pots
in the kitchen

could be used to summon
anything I desired and I made it
summon lavender and irises,
roses and mugwort so I could

keep making my potions.
Once I poured a concoction
onto the floors and turned
the onyx into pristine marble.

Pallas laughed, but Styx
was not pleased at all since
she did not like my experiments.
She thought they would draw attention

from the strange things
that occupied this realm.
The trouble was I was restless.
I still thought of my parents.

The cruel fate of my mother.
The sad eyes of my father.
I had made a promise when
I saw him in Tartarus.

I would free him.
And it was a promise

I intended to keep,
but I could not do that from here.

Palace walls spoke no answers.
And it was not long
before I found myself
walking back into Asphodel.

As I walked that day
through the meadows,
the scent of lavender
mixing with mist.

I heard the sound of
reuniting families.
Brother meeting brother,
sisters together again,

fathers seeing their sons,
but the pull I felt most
was towards the women
still waiting for their loved ones.

Women who were all alone
but, like the North Star,
shone like celestial bodies
in these grey fields.

Every War Had Them

The women who got here first.
Some of them were scarcely more than girls.
Others wore maps of memory across
their aged skin, long silver hair cascading
like water down their backs.

They found one another in these fields,
learned to make families out of each other
when their own loved ones were nowhere
to be found. I know this because in those
early days, I had grown close to the ways

of the spirits inside these meadows.
Styx may not have understood this yet,
but I had learned to be observant
as all children of dark situations do.
So I watched at first as the women

gathered and sat together in circles.
I watched as they told stories
and sang songs from where they came.
It was these vibrant tales and lyrics
that drew me closer to them every day.

And when one day
I was finally close enough,
they did not fall silent.
Instead, they simply shifted
and made space in their circle for me.

Tales From Across the World

These circles were rich with folklore,
and they held such vibrant stories and songs.
Some of them were about the bloodshed,
but others were about happier times,
childhoods spent chasing the sun and
girlhoods spent dreaming in the moonlight.

There were other tales, too, of Goddesses
from the new ruling family of Olympians.
The fury of Hera but also her kindness
to women during childbirth.
The might of Athena but also her partiality
for heroes above all else.

I absorbed everything about this ruling family
of Gods from these women.
The Olympians were the reason why
my mother was now an island far away.
They were the reason why my father
and his brothers were trapped in Tartarus.

But the women also gave me stories of kings
and their queens, farmers and artists.
Their great loves and great conquests
all won and gone in the blink of an eye.
Everything seemed so much more finite
when you were mortal.
Everything ached more, hurt more.
If you are doomed from the start,
you learn to savour every drop of life
in ways immortals never can.

On Love

Sometimes I would wonder about it.
When the oldest of women
and even the youngest of maids
would speak about a lover.

They would unravel tales
that would make me blush.
Stories about stolen kisses
and moonlight walks

which would make me think of
him again. The boy with kind
and tired eyes. The way he had
seen an ache in me and answered it

by showing me how to gain
the trust of the biggest of beasts.
The way he saw a loneliness in me
that spoke to him where I couldn't.

I wondered if I would ever see him
again. I wondered why I wanted to.
But the more stories I heard,
the brighter and more lovely

his face and kindness became.

The Crone

She was the oldest story Asphodel had to offer. The whisper passed from ghost to ghost said that she had walked here for decades. Longer than I had been in the Underworld, longer, it is said, than Hades or even Styx had been. She was glimpsed walking only by the fortunate few and they all said the same of her: she was seeking someone. Someone she had never found. Her long white hair fell to her ankles. She wore a black shroud and carried a wooden cane, its handle smooth under her wizened hands. She kept her distance, never approaching any of the spirits who walked here. So when she appeared before me one day, I remembered Styx's words about the strange, terrifying beings and my heart thudded at her proximity to me. Where her pupils were meant to be, there was milk-white nothingness, and yet it still felt like she was staring into my soul. When she sensed me, she smiled and said, 'It is you, keeper of the crossroads.' I shook my head, confused by her words. 'I am just Hekate,' I told her quietly. She nodded slowly, 'Yes. Hekate, the keeper of the crossroads. I have a tale for you.' I wanted to run because that was what every bone in my body was telling me to do. But her words made me curious. And stories had become my only way to know this unusual realm I lived in. It was the offer of a story that made me stay. Instead of running, I simply nodded and sat down among the asphodel-grey flowers and lavender to listen.

A Fable of Gods and Monsters

The endings of wars are just as painful as beginnings. When you survey the damage left in the aftermath, a blood-drenched battlefield is the least of your concerns. And so, when the Titanomachy came to an end, ten thousand years of ichor lost, the old Gods, the Titans, imprisoned in their volcanic dungeon, their wives and daughters taken from them by the new Gods, the Olympians, Zeus, the God-King of this new empire, realized that to reinforce their immortality, something more would be needed. But he did not want to rule through fear the way his father had; he wanted to be a better ruler than Kronos ever was. And so Prometheus, the cosmic creator and Zeus' oldest friend, invented the new mortals, to worship and empower the Olympians. Kronos' mortals had been too placid, too strong, too clever. You see, child, prayer is what keeps Gods powerful. What good is immortality if you cannot call upon immense forces at whim? The mortals were taught to pray and to birth more like themselves who would continue those prayers. And those prayers kept the altars of the Gods perpetually fragranced with sweet-smelling smoke. For a while, this delicately crafted system worked. But the mortals grew restless. Like the Gods, they wanted more. Palaces to live in. Bigger fields. A perpetual, abundant crop. Their unhappy voices grew stronger until the Gods could no longer ignore them. So for the mortals, they appointed kings and queens, inventing a hierarchy that allowed some mortals to rise over others. And yet, the majority remained unhappy. Infuriated with their insolence, the Gods invented fear. Monsters were the first of their creations to inspire terror. They crafted terrible beasts to harm mortals and demolish villages until each mortal king appointed a God-blessed hero to save them. Famines. Floods. Fires. If the Gods could not have prayer through peace, then they would have it through fear. And on this occasion, their plan worked. So now these same Gods, who said they were different from the old order, ruled by the same fear that Zeus swore he would never rule by. And the monsters they sent to Earth, to harm mortals in their name, paid the ultimate price. For even though every monster fulfilled its exact purpose of what the Gods invented it for, they were named villains and their eternal fate was to be hunted by heroes chosen by the Gods. There is no difference between Gods and monsters, child. Each, in their own way, wields their power to terrorize.

'And Precisely What Are You Doing Here?'

I knew from the cold spike
that laced those words
it was Styx, her voice
full of controlled anger.

I turned to her and smiled,
a gesture I knew
would infuriate her.
'I was listening to a story.'

A frown marred her face
as she looked at me, then past me.
Her words were measured as she asked,
'And who was telling you this story?'

I turned to where she was looking
but my heart already knew.
The crone was gone
as though she had never

been there at all.

Charon Visited

He knew he shouldn't. I had been
forbidden from seeing anyone
after my last escapade in Asphodel.
Styx was furious I had disobeyed her.

It was also, I had now learned, at risk to himself.
If Hades learned of his visits,
he could burn the oak of his handcrafted ferry.
Yet it was the only way Charon could see me.

And besides, he told me,
he could make himself another boat.
But I knew it was not that simple.
He was the ferryman and it was his duty

to escort the dead where they must go.
A boat to carry the dead was crafted
in the dangerous bowels of the Underworld
with the blessing of Hades himself.

It warmed my heart that he would do this,
risk the wrath of Styx and Hades
to see me, and for our friendship.
So as he sat there at my obsidian table,

our laughing reflections gleaming
inside the smooth surface,
torches around us
glowing with light,

I listened carefully as he told me
about his day, his work and sometimes now,

he confided in me of the difficulty of growing up
as a bright son of the darkness and the night.

'So,' he asked,
'why has Styx forbidden you
from even leaving the palace?
What have you done?'

'Nothing,' I said abruptly. But he
raised his eyebrows and I relented.
'I was in Asphodel some days ago
and I met an old woman.'

Charon's eyes narrowed.
'Was she in a black shroud?'
I nodded.
'And did she have no eyes?'

I nodded again
and was greeted with silence.
Then I noticed Charon
had sat back in his seat.

Finally, at long last,
he spoke,
his words like
cold metal and ice.

'The woman you met
was a Goddess, a Moirai.
She is the oldest
of the three Fates.'

'What Are the Moirai?'

I asked this out of fear
and because I had never seen
Charon so serious.

Our friendship was made of
laughter and stories,
and to see him like this . . .

He reached across the table
and grasped my hand.
'The Fates are dangerous,

Hekate. They answer to no one.
Promise me that you will never
talk to them again.'

His hand gripped mine hard
and I frowned at his words.
'But what are they?'

'They control the divine order.
Who lives, who dies.
They spin the threads

of all our lives.'
I was surprised by this,
'Even the Gods?'

He nodded. 'Even the Gods.
Even Ferryman Gods like me.'
Mentions of his divinity

always made him uncomfortable,
so he continued as though
he had not mentioned

his divine role at all.
'They are above Gods,
men and monsters alike.

They sit next to Hades
in his palace so he can
keep a watchful eye on them.'

My frown deepened.
'So because they answer to no one
they are dangerous?'

Charon shook his head.
'They are more so
. . . unpredictable.'

Something about his words
made me draw my hand back.
It seemed to me

that anything unpredictable
was named dangerous
by Gods and men alike.

But the word 'unpredictable'
seemed reserved
for women alone.

'A woman they cannot control,
whether Goddess or mortal,
is a dangerous woman.'

My mother once told me this.
I was beginning to understand precisely
what she meant by those words.

But there was something else.
Something within Charon's words.
If the Moirai were above Gods,

would they know every God
and mortal's destiny
and what they were here for?

'I Thought I Said No Visitors, Hekate'

Charon and I both turned to see Styx
. . . but something was wrong.

Pallas had a protective arm around her
and she rested her head on his shoulder.

'We bring news,' he said quietly,
and for a terrible moment, I thought

that Styx may cry. Instead, she moved
her head from his shoulder and said,

'I think it is news that should be shared
with a cup of wine.' She walked to the kitchen

as Charon raised an eyebrow and I frowned
in deep confusion. She always told me

I was too young to drink wine.
But she reappeared with four cups

and placed one before each of us
before the wine rose and poured itself.

'It's about Prometheus,' Styx said.
Prometheus the clever was our cousin

who had invented mortals out of clay.
He had sided with the Olympians,

even though he was a Titan, and now
held the position of Zeus' closest friend

and confidant. We waited for Styx to explain
what had happened. But when she didn't,

Pallas slowly told us, 'Prometheus stole
Zeus' divine fire to give to his beloved mortals.

And when Zeus found out, he punished him.'
His voice broke slightly and he took

a long sip of wine. Charon and I waited
for him to continue. He put his cup down.

'Zeus had him brought to his halls,
chained to a pillar and whipped till he bled.'

A gasp escaped my throat, but Pallas
continued, 'He made us all watch.

And when it was done and Prometheus
lay bleeding, he had him bound to a rock

on the mountains and his liver was eaten
by Zeus' eagle.' My stomach sickened at this

but Pallas was not finished.
'Every night, his liver will grow back

only to be eaten again.'
A long, numb silence followed.

'Was what he did so awful?'
I asked in a small, trembling voice.

Styx spoke softly, 'It was not
what he did, but who he did it to.'

Charon's eyes flashed as he looked up.
'It was a message for the rest of us.'

'Charon,' Pallas warned quietly,
but my friend simply glared.

'Tell me this is not a message from Zeus?
Tell me that this was not to warn

any Titan who works against an Olympian
that they will be destroyed in the worst way?'

Neither Pallas nor Styx spoke.
And I knew then that the war

may have ended, but Zeus still saw
every single one of us as a threat to his reign.

That Night My Sleep Was Fitful

I dreamed all night of Prometheus,
stealing fire for mortals because
they were cold and hungry and

what father could watch his children
starve? I dreamed of him standing
before Zeus, refusing to beg for mercy,

the God-King ordering him whipped
for every Olympian and Titan to see.
And then it was not Prometheus,

but my father's face, and it was he
who Zeus was punishing,
And had dragged away from me

And I woke up
screaming,

screaming,

screaming.

Nightmares

For days these terrible dreams
plagued me till visions formed in my mind.
My father's face and my promise to him
haunted my waking days now.
Madness felt close. Too close.

I was desperate enough to try
anything. Anything to help me
keep this fear and helplessness at bay.
Something to occupy my mind and body.
So I took ink and paper and began

to fill them with the stories
from Asphodel, from Charon,
the tales Pallas brought from his travels.
In my mind, I became
the keeper of all these fables.

And for a while, this worked.

The Awareness

formed slowly. As the edges of my mind
frayed with a madness that haunted me,
still picturing my father's face,
I began to see strange threads
in all of the stories.

Purpose. Every story had a purpose.
Every tale led to a destination.
Every mortal life came to an ending.
Immortals have no endings.
But every God should have a purpose,

one our fathers are meant to bless us with
at the very beginning of our lives.
And that was when, like a rich tapestry,
the threads came together.
I needed to go to see the Moirai.

I needed to see them before my madness
consumed me and left me a husk of myself.
The question was, how would I get there?
Charon had said that the Fates would be
inside Hades' palace in his throne room.

That was a place into which
even the bravest of heroes
would not venture.
But I was no hero.
And I had nothing left to lose.

The Palace of Hades

was deep in the heart of the Underworld.
It was said to be a thing of both beauty
and great fear.

The towers were made of volcanic glass,
cooled from Tartarus
where my father was held captive.

Onyx halls gleamed
with a blood-red moon's glow
that lit up the torches.

It was said that on the eve of curses
and wars, Hades cast this bloody gleam
across the moon as warning.

It was also said his throne was made
of bones and skulls from the evillest of mortals
pieced together.

They said every mortal soul
that made up this throne
was forever trapped in agony.

It was this room I had to visit
if I was to meet the Fates,
and ask them . . . what?

I did not know. I just knew, I must go.

Hades

was no longer the boy-God I remembered,
the one who led me to my father,
gave me protection from his own brothers,
felt the same pain in the aftermath of war
that I did.

Instead, when he visited Styx,
I saw a God carrying heavy responsibilities.
He eyed me with suspicion for reasons
I could not fathom and when he spoke to Styx,
he talked only of duties.

His face too was different,
the innocent gleam of the boy-God
inside his eyes had given way
to the darkness of an ancient burden.
'The dead are eternal,' he told Styx bitterly,

'and therefore I am an eternal ruler
with eternal tasks.' I imagined this,
a God whose duties were never done,
a task list as immortal as him,
and to be alone through all of it.

Styx watched him leave with some sorrow.
'The crown is tempting to all,'
she murmured softly, 'other than
the one who must wear it.'
It was true. I had never heard a story

of a truly happy king or queen.
Their lives seemed to always lead
to tragedy in some way,

whether through war
or fear of losing that poisoned crown.

'It is no wonder that getting to his palace
is a task so difficult,' Styx muttered darkly
as she dipped her feet back into her river,
preparing to disappear.
'A drawbridge to a cypress tree,

finding the key to Elysium,
all the way through Nyx's realm,
and if you manage all that
you must avoid the Gods in Grey.
It's a wonder how anyone visits him at all.'

Perhaps that is the point,
I thought as I watched her leave.
If you keep only your own company
it is much harder to lose your crown.
But now I wondered

if I was caught trying to get into
the palace of this new Hades,
if it would be seen as nothing short
of treason in his increasingly
paranoid eyes.

And this was only the first
of my many, many hurdles.

The Gods in Grey

The Underworld echoed with old stories.
Many of these stories were simply rumours
but it was difficult to tell the difference
between legend and lore.

But this one? This legend made sense.
You see, it was a straight path
from the lavender-dipped
Asphodel Meadows,

through the orchard of dark fruit
that belonged to Hades,
beyond which lay
his palace.

But what protected Hades' palace
were beings so unfathomably brutal
we only knew them as
the Gods in Grey.

It was said that
they were manifestations
of shadows and evil thoughts,
dark deeds and cruelty.

Once these things terrorized
the Gods and mortals so much
that they were imprisoned
in Tartarus, locked away forever by Zeus.

But Hades made a bargain with them.
Freedom from Tartarus in exchange

for their guardianship of his palace.
They swore an oath to him by Styx's waters.

If they caught you . . .
no one knew what happened.
There were no survivors
to tell that tale.

A Dangerous Idea

But even the stories of the Gods in Grey
did not deter me or cause me any fear.
When your fear is an existential threat
like the Olympians, or madness from
never being able to rescue either
of your parents, other fears seem
trivial before it.

I filled a big flask with nectar.
I put together a bag of simples,
the few herbs and flowers that
I had managed to turn into
something useful. I added
the map I had been creating.
And then began to consider Cerberus,
the guardian of the gate.

I could take him some game,
but I knew his skill at smelling
intention. It was his preternatural power
to be able to tell the purpose
of every visitor to the Underworld.
If he guessed I was going beyond
the Asphodel Meadows,
he may alert Hades.

And that would not do.
Inside the game I gave him
there must be a sleeping potion.

When I Went to See Cerberus Now

he was always happy to see me.
His long tail thumped so hard
on the ground that it made
the ground quake under me.

I smiled at his three large faces,
still unsure which one to look at,
but all three were lowering themselves
in my direction, hoping for a pat.

The lesson the kind-eyed boy
had given me stayed with me.
As I thought of him, I felt a pang,
wondering if I would see him again.

I stroked each soft snout gently
and told Cerberus, 'Good dog,'
then I pulled out the three pieces
of enchanted game from

my worn leather satchel
and placed them on the ground.
As he snacked and his eyes began to close,
I quietly moved to the gleaming light

that spilled between those
stone doors
and pushed them hard.
They opened

just enough for me to slip through.
I was distracting him with food

and my magics, I knew this.
But all creatures respond well to trust.

Even monster dogs.

Advice From My Mother

When my mother and I were on the run
I remember her telling me,
'Always bring a guide with you
everywhere you go.'

At the time I thought a guide meant
another immortal like us,
or even a mortal who knew
where to go.

But my years under the earth's surface
in a strange unland forbidden
to earthly mortals and sky-dwelling
Gods had taught me that a guide

could be made from parchment,
darkening ink, a sense of adventure,
the power of observation and
a knowledge of stories.

How to Navigate the Underworld

My makeshift map told me everything I needed to know. I was to cross the Stygian Marsh, the acrid, quicksand marsh Styx's river left just before the Asphodel Meadows. Here I had confidence, as I had done this countless times before with the help of carefully laid stones across the marshes. At the end of the asphodel flora and the lavender were three nameless mountains. The one in the centre would give way to Hades' vast orchards of blackened and golden fruit. Just beyond the orchard was his palace guarded by the Gods in Grey. So I would take the mountain to the right instead. If what Charon had told me of this place held true, I would have to cross a long, uneven drawbridge over Lethe, the river of oblivion, to get to the cypress tree, which protected the entrance to the Elysian Fields, the realm of the righteous where all the heroes went. It was dangerous, but if I wanted to see the three Fates, it was less dangerous than the path through Hades' orchard, for I was sure to get caught by the Gods in Grey there. Crossing the Elysian Fields would give me safe passage towards the Realm of Night, ruled by Nyx, the Goddess of the Night, and her darkling children. It was from here I would need to request safe passage to guide me into the Palace of Hades. There is no Goddess in the world quite like Nyx. Whether Titan or Olympian, every God fears her. But Goddesses have always been welcomed into her realm. At least according to Styx's stories and Charon's legends. I hoped, for my own sake, that they were true.

The Beginning of a Quest

As I slipped past a sleeping Cerberus
since he ate the meat I gave him,
and treaded the stones over
the Stygian Marsh past the door,
my heart thudded with excitement.

A feeling of adventure
washed over me
as I walked past spirits
telling each other tales
of lives long gone.

I breathed in the comfort
of the cold mist
that I had come to know so well.
Asphodel felt like home,
where I had spent a strange childhood

surrounded by kind, ghostly
women who raised me
with their stories and
never questioned why
an immortal child visited them.

Now, as I reached
the cobalt mountain to the right,
I hesitated at the doorway to the unknown.
I knew once I crossed that threshold
there would be no turning back.

But I thought of the madness.
The promise I had made
that I would free my father.

All that I was seeking
that could not be found

in those palace walls.
My mind sharpened with
determination. Then
I laid my fingers on the ancient
mountain's stone doors

and pushed.

Lethe

The stone doors gave way to ice-blue walls.
As my eyes adjusted I realized I was inside
a mountain cave of bright blue quartz
that reflected the river's light from below.

The river was far beneath where I stood,
the two sides connected by a bridge that went
all the way through the mountain,
far beyond my line of sight.

From the river rose tendrils of smoke
that looked just like the Asphodel mists,
but I knew better from Charon.
Those tendrils were not mists, but memories.

Lethe was where ghosts who were once
mortals were taken to forget everything,
and her waters were potent with pain,
grief, but also joy and happiness.

They say she did not differentiate between
mortals and Gods. That anyone who drank
from these waters lost their memories
now and forevermore.

The Drawbridge

did not look sturdy.
In fact it did not look safe at all.
But if Styx's story was correct,
I knew I must follow it.
All the way to the cypress tree.

I could not turn back now.

So I took a deep breath
as the rush of Lethe deafened me,
and started to walk pace after pace
on the damp oak planks,
trying not to look down

at the gush of oblivion below.

Twice

I almost slipped.
The drawbridge rocked
dangerously as I crossed it.
I was not unsteady on my feet,

> but it was not often that anything
> living crossed this bridge.
> It was clearly built
> as an afterthought.

The second time I stumbled,
I nearly slipped through the planks.
It was by sheer luck my fingers
grasped the rope and I pulled myself up.

> I wanted to turn back then,
> but instead, I looked up at the mountain walls
> and saw the glisten of the blue quartz
> shine down at me like sapphires.

'Go on,' they seemed to urge me.
'You are so close, go on.'
So I steeled myself
and took the next step.

> Then the next and the next, but then . . .

The Thing on the Drawbridge

It was standing in the middle
of the drawbridge.

Initially I thought it was a mortal spirit
lost, seeking some kind of path

but the pale, white, naked form
gave me pause. Its arms were

too long and its legs too long,
and then it turned . . .

and it had no face.
I froze, my blood cold

with a fear I had never felt before.
And then . . . it began to run towards me.

I panicked and tried to turn
and run but the thing was

shaking the bridge too much
and though I held the sides

of the ropes and tried to keep
my balance, I slipped and fell

through the cracks in the drawbridge
and as the river raced beneath me

and I watched in horror
as the thing drew nearer and nearer,

I tried my best to pull myself up
and just as my hand slipped—

Two Hands Grasped Me

And I screeched as I felt my body
lifted away from the edge
until I was so high above the drawbridge
it looked like a toy beneath my feet.

The creature down below raised its arms
as though trying to catch me,
but it was too late, I was too far up
for it to reach me.

I turned to see the mischievous face of a boy
wearing a wide-brimmed traveller's hat.
But the strange thing about this hat
was that it had wings.

Hermes

When they spoke of the Gods,
Hermes was the one always
associated with laughter.
His wit was legendary,
he was a trickster, a deceiver.

As just a baby, he had outwitted Apollo,
his own brother the Sun God,
by making a meal of Apollo's favourite cows,
turning their insides into a lyre
for the Sun God who loved music.

As he got older still,
he aided Zeus in hiding from Hera,
cleverly ensuring his place
among the Olympians as much more
than a messenger God.

Hermes knew from an early age
how to be crafty enough for posterity.
And yet, it was for precisely this reason
I had to wonder why he would possibly
want to save or protect me?

The Cypress Tree

A thing this alive should
not grow among the dead.

I thought this to myself as Hermes landed
and let me go. My legs trembled on solid ground,

if that is what it could be called.
The soil was damp and full of ancient roots.

For a moment all I could do was look around.
The blue quartz of the mountain had receded

and was replaced by golden amber crystals
wedged into the inner walls of this cavern.

The river ended here under this tree
and began here too as it circled the mountain.

An ouroboros of water, the snake eating itself,
I thought to myself as I watched

the way the river light struck the amber crystals,
making them look lit from within.

And in turn they made the gold leaves
of the cypress tree glisten,

and Hermes' tawny eyes danced
like a stolen sun glowed within them.

'Hekate.' His smile made his boyish face
look like a much younger child's.

'I was hoping that we would meet one day.
It appears that day is today.'

He tilted his head and his cap slipped
slightly to a crooked angle,

only adding to his charm.
'Now my question is:

does Styx know you are here
crossing the River Lethe?'

Secrets

Hermes was part of the ruling family of Olympians,
and if there was one thing I had learned
about the eternal ruling family,
it was that one must never be dull.

This was especially true with Hermes.
So with my answer, I also carried a smirk
drenched in the nectar of a confidence
I did not have and yet came easily.

'I thank you for your protection,'
I said smoothly, choosing
my words with great caution.

'But why should I trust the trickster God
with any of my intentions or secrets?'
His eyes gleamed with a joyful mischief.
'Oh so it *is* a secret then, is it?'

He dropped his voice to a theatrical whisper.
'I will simply have to guess what it is.'
There was careful wielding of power here;
his face was open with laughter

but even I knew better than to cross
the God of Boundaries.

'And Why Are You Here?'

The question escaped my lips
before I could even stop it.
It hung there out of my reach.

Hermes seemed surprised,
almost as though he wasn't
asked this often.

'Do you not know, young one,
that I am what they call
a psychopompos?'

A psychopompos,
Charon had told me,
is a guide to the dead.

'And who are you guiding?'
I asked, looking behind him.
'I see no one with you.'

'I too can keep a secret,'
he said cryptically,
then gestured beyond the cypress.

'Shall we?' he asked,
and with a fluid flick of his fingers,
golden light poured like magma

from the mountainside
closest to us, spilling away
into the River Lethe.

The Golden Doorway

I turned to watch his clever,
cat-like eyes studying me.

'How did you do that?'
I asked in complete awe.

'My uncle gave me a key.'
He shrugged, walking towards

the amber doorway.
Uncle. I thought. *Hades*.

The transparent, gold-hued glass
revealed . . . *Paradise*.

Entry

Hermes held his hand out and I stared at it. His skin was beautiful, smooth like the oaken chair my mother loved so well when we once had a palace. Seeing my hesitation, he gestured open-handed at the soft leather satchel I was carrying, which contained my map and nectar. 'You cannot carry this inside with you.' My fingers clutched my bag. 'I am going nowhere without this.' Seeing the mischief in his eyes, I made sure that Hermes heard the edge of fire in my voice. He did not push me further; instead, raised his palm out towards the door. It opened easily for him, the amber giving way to gleaming sunshine. The only place in all of the Underworld that was allowed to be touched by the sun were these blessed islands. It occurred to me that paradise existed both here, deep within the earth's rock, but also in the world above, reflecting upon the salty waters of the mortals' deathless sea, for what is paradise without the sun? I wondered what divine ancient granted this for just Elysium, what law of celestial spaces allowed it to exist in two places at once? But as Hermes stepped through the doors, his silhouette illuminated in sunlight I had not seen since I was a child, all thoughts escaped me. Taking a deep breath, I stepped into the golden rays of the sun.

The Elysian Fields

When I was still new to the Underworld, Styx had told me her waters did not reach the blessed islands and this was why she could never bring me here. Now I think there was another reason. The thought of Styx, ancient, pale and lover of all dark things, even setting foot in this place seemed laughable. As the veil dropped from my eyes to reveal the island in all its glory, the sun warmed my forever cool skin. Sweet birdsong glowed across the lush green valleys and hills. Across the vast expanse of land, I saw groves of abundant trees heavy with golden and crimson fruit rivalling those I once ate as a child. Gentle cows, soft rabbits and playful goats roamed freely across rolling fields. And the flowers! Soft grey, white, azure, ruby, every colour you could imagine, forever in youthful bloom. Past the valleys as I shielded my eyes, I saw the turquoise, light-flecked waters of the open seas. So this was what paradise, true paradise, was meant to be. I turned to Hermes and saw that he was watching me carefully, a smile wide across his face. 'We will find Cadmus and Harmonia. I am sure they will be glad to meet you.'

Cadmus and Harmonia

To believe there was such a time
before they knew each other
felt as impossible as these islands,

but such a time did exist.
Once, Cadmus had been on a quest
seeking out his lost sister, stolen by Zeus.

The same Zeus who was grandfather
to Harmonia, Goddess of Harmony and Concord.
This should have complicated matters.

It did not. Instead, Cadmus and Harmonia
fell in love and where one went
the other would not be far behind,

through cursed jewels,
the slaying of sacred dragons
and the fall of a kingdom.

So the legend goes that when Cadmus
was cursed to become a serpent,
Harmonia begged for the same fate.

They were both brought here,
a love so strong that even the Gods
could not bear to separate them.

But what did Hermes want with them?

The Meeting

Hermes spoke as we walked.
'I take it that you will not be here long.'

I shook my head.
'I am passing through to the Halls of Night.'

A frown marred his childlike features.
'Are you aware of what lies there?'

I nodded carefully.
'Yes, I have heard the stories.'

When he said nothing,
I tore my eyes away from

a meadow of blood-red flowers
to look at his perplexed expression.

His tone was quiet and measured.
'What is it, Hekate, that you seek?'

I could not tell him. The war may have been over,
but even the dead sometimes spoke

about the eternal resentments
the Gods bore towards each other.

One wrong word, and the Olympian
in him would be unleashed.

Before I Could Speak

I saw something move.
When I turned to look
at what it was, my body
turned entirely rigid.

At first glance it looked like
a strange rock on the hill,
but on closer inspection,
I realized that these

were the glittering scales
of not one but two serpents.
Terrifyingly large, they raised
their flat heads, split eyes

trained upon me and Hermes.
And then, slowly, they began
to glide their enormous
bodies down the hill

towards us, tongues flickering,
their massive fangs visible
even from this distance,
as Hermes waved to them.

Divine Serpents

I knew I should not be afraid,
but the serpents resembled a Hydra,
a terrible snake-headed monster
that only a son of Zeus could defeat,
and fear rattled inside my bones.

The closer they got, the bigger
they seemed, and the carvings
on their long, slithering bodies
were curious enough that I asked
Hermes, 'What are those markings?'

Hermes' soft, mocking laugh
warmed the air. 'Where have they
been hiding you in Hades,
that you have not heard about this?
Those carvings are their love story.

They were given to them as a gift
of their enduring, immortal love.'
What a strange gift, I thought.
A lasting brand of their punishment
for loving each other so much.

The Voices of Serpents

What startled me was that,
though they were serpents now,
they had not forgotten
their divine voices,
nor how to use them,

and so I stepped back in shock
when Cadmus spoke.
'Welcome, old friend,'
he addressed Hermes,
'I trust your journey was safe?'

The corner of Hermes' mouth lifted
in a crooked smile towards me.
'For me, it was good as always.
I even gathered a cousin
as a companion on the journey.'

At this, Harmonia's glittering eyes
turned to me, 'And you, child?
I can see the golden Titanide
in you. Was your mother Mnemosyne?
Or are you the child of Tethys of the water?'

It was hard for me to say
my mother's name. The rush
of pain that filled my throat forced me
to speak it in less cadence, more croak.
'I am Asteria's child. My name is Hekate.'

Cadmus and Harmonia
looked at one another and
an unreadable thought exchanged.

Then, with a hiss, Harmonia whispered,
'You are welcome here,
child of War and Falling Stars.'

An Eternal Day

We sat together upon soft grass,
The sea breeze upon our skin and scales,

and they serenaded each other with wit.
Cadmus talked about his bygone days

travelling across the oceans with his kin,
seeking out his lost sister. He was mortal.

Harmonia spoke of growing up in the halls
of a palace long since ash. She was a Goddess.

It always struck me as odd when Gods
allowed their immortal progeny to marry

mortals. It almost always ended in heartache.
But if the Olympians had not granted Harmonia's wish,

she would have wandered Earth and sky
with a broken heart, driven to despair.

Hermes regaled us with tales of his travels.
None, I noticed, of his family at Olympus.

As for me, when they finally turned my way,
I had nothing to offer them. So, I gave them

instead, the only thing I could.
A thought I had been too afraid to even say aloud.

"I am on a quest to know my destiny.
I want to know what I am here for."

The Caduceus

At my declaration, Hermes turned
to Cadmus and Harmonia.
'It is time.' The two slowly rose,
serpent heads moving hypnotically.

Hermes had put a polished, oak staff
between them. 'Prometheus' last gift,'
he said softly, his eyes on the staff.
Our uncle of invention punished for his rebellion.

Without waiting for any more instructions,
Cadmus and Harmonia slithered
towards the staff and, moving
like they were dancing,

swirled their bodies around it
till they were a perfect, symmetrical
pair facing each other.
Something about it made me feel

unwell, like something awful
was about to happen,
something unchangeable,
and my stomach lurched.

Hermes' fingers reached out
to grip the end of the staff
and at his touch,
much like Midas,

the serpents suddenly became
shockingly still, as still as
the dead as their bodies
turned into cold, metallic gold.

Shock Flooded My Body

'*Hermes, what have you done?!*'
I stared at the staff and tried to take it.

He held it away from my grasp,
'I did what my friends asked me to do.'

This is what Olympians do,
I chided myself. I was so foolish,

trusting him as I had.
'Your friends asked you to—'

'They were tired of this place,'
Hermes told me, looking at the staff.

'Tired?' I asked him, gesturing
to a forever glen flooded with sunshine.

'They want to travel. This place,
it has dulled.' Hermes looked at me.

'Dulled,' I repeated softly, thinking.
Perhaps he was right.

There were few joys to be had
if you were a deathless thing.

If novelty did not visit you,
you must invent it.

'We Must Leave Now'

It was not that I did not expect his words.
It was simply that they came so abruptly
after the life-shaking transformation.

He was already on his feet, looking at me.
'We must reach the falls of night soon,
before they start seeking you out.'

He was right. If Styx visited my palace
and I was not within its obsidian walls,
she would first visit the Asphodel Meadows.

And, unable me to find me there,
she would think something had taken me
and send word to Hades

that I had disappeared, and even I
did not want to risk the wrath of Hades.
They said the most placid of Gods

hid the worst hurricanes
inside their divine blood.
I got to my feet and followed Hermes.

Across the Eternal

As we walked through the glen
Hermes talked. I realized he did this
because he could not bear silence.
Perhaps this was why the halls of Olympus

with their constant chatter and rumours
suited him so very well. The only change
in his demeanour came when I reached
for a golden fruit hanging from a tree.

Before I could raise it to my mouth,
his hand was on mine, quick as lightning.
'Even Gods do not eat fruit from Elysium.'

It was a simple instruction but there was
an edge in his voice that demanded obedience.
When he looked away
I pocketed the fruit to examine later.

We walked for so long that I had to stop
and take a drink of nectar.
Hermes took the flask from my hands
without asking and drank long and deep.

I said nothing. I was slowly learning
that this was his nature. He drank
the whole world deeply, as if it belonged
to him.
For the Olympians did own
this whole world and everything in it, at least,

for now.

The Falls of Night

At last we were at a waterfall
somewhere in the middle

of the grassy glen surrounded
by a copse of evergreen trees.

The dark rush of the waterfall
fell into a lake so black

that it looked like the night sky,
and the ripples from the cascade

resembled soft clouds.
Flecks of silver shone up,

the scales of the fish looked
so much like the stars.

I turned to Hermes.
'Where is the doorway?'

He pointed to the top
of the waterfall.

I stared up but only saw
the azure sky.

'I don't see it.'
He shook his head.

'You must go to the edge
and then jump.'

My eyes widened
and I looked at him.

'I must . . . jump?'
He nodded gravely.

'The Falls of Night
are a game of trust.'

Trust

I did not know what kind of game this was, but I had heard a hundred stories of Gods who liked to play strange games. Trickster Gods like Hermes and clever Goddesses like Hera who did not spare any divinity or mortal. My skin prickled under his gaze as we climbed the moly-covered hill to the top of the waterfall. There was no river that led to it, it looked like it started from a large, moss-covered rock. Hermes smiled at me. 'Nyx made the doorway to her realm deliberately difficult. The Goddess of the Night is not welcoming to strangers in her home, she does not like any intrusions on her peace. This includes all divinities other than her own children.' I knew well what I was risking trying to cross through the Halls of the Night. But it was the only path I could use to get to Mnemosyne, the river of memory. The water would take me to the Forest of Silence, which I shuddered to think of, but at the other end of the forest lay my destination, the Palace of Hades. It seemed an impossible path. But every light I have ever seen has been on the other side of darkness.

'You Must Take the Cave to the Night Realm'

Hermes' voice was careful.
But I could hear something else.
Was it perhaps concern?

'You should know,'
he said, as though
reading my mind,

'even I do not pass
through that realm.
Nyx is a law unto her own.'

Through the ivy of fear
that was crowding my heart,
these words gleamed

like a gold coin
shimmering among stones.
An ancient Goddess

so formidable that even
Olympians feared her.
What power that must be.

I looked back at the waters
and suddenly,
they seemed more inviting.

So I waded through them
to the rock where they started
from and climbed up.

'I Hope Fortune Favours You'

The words were called in earnest
and I turned to Hermes now,
just to take in the last of him.

His gleaming cap with wings,
his brand new staff
and the mischief in his smile.

'Thank you, Hermes.'
I never thought that
I would thank an Olympian

but I would have never
found this lake without him.
Hermes lifted his fist as a gesture

of good will and with
kindness in his voice
spoke gently,

'Go with grace, Cousin.'
It was true we came from the same family,
but how different our paths.

And yet he had been kind to me
so I nodded and smiled at him.
I took a deep breath, my whole body

steeling itself that this was the point of no return.
I thought of my parents and their courage.
And then, I turned to the edge

and jumped.

A Fall

The shock of icy waters
hit my body first.

Warmed by the Elysian sun,
I had forgotten cold

almost entirely
until this moment.

And when I opened my eyes,
all I could see was darkness

like a night with no stars
and no glowing moon.

But still, something
pulled at my feet

dragging me down
through the waters

as though hooks
had been threaded

through my ankles.
For the first time

I thanked my immortality.
For at least I could breathe

underwater.

And a Pull

At some point the fall
became a pull upwards.

It started at my waist,
as though the claws

of some great creature
had wrapped around me

and were drawing me up
to meet its eye.

My limbs were like a doll's
floating uselessly

as the force pulled
until through the inky dark

I finally saw the light.
And then, just as abruptly

as I had fallen in,
I was out of the water,

tossed inelegantly
onto a rocky ground.

When my eyes cleared
I saw the light reflected first

and then as I turned . . .

I Saw the Caves

There were two.
One next to where I lay
still gasping,
a host of yellow glowing
crystals mounted along the walls.

The second past
the small pool
I emerged from,
an abyss pitch dark
and unwelcoming.

Hermes did not warn me
that there would be two.
I looked down
into the water
and only saw my own face.

There was nothing there
to tell me which way
I should go.
But one had gemstone light,
a way to see.

As I look back on this
it was clear enough
that cave was not
the place to go. And yet . . .
it was the one I chose.

By the Light of Gemstones

My reasoning at the time
was rooted in logic.
Light led the way,
whereas darkness hid
any path that lay ahead.

So as I followed the crystal light,
carefully avoiding the teeth-like
minerals growing up from the cave floor,
I noticed that along
the uneven walls of rocks,

there were paintings.
The colours were warm,
rich purples and bright yellows,
crimson and vermillion.
But the paintings were . . .

I shuddered as I looked upon them.
They were clearly of battle.
A brutality shone in the swords,
the bodies of Gods and Goddesses
being ripped to shreds.

Even on these uneven walls,
I could see how violently
the artist's brush had slashed,
creating clear images
of every cruelty of war.

And then my stomach
turned as I realized
with a cold shock

that these images
were of the Titanomachy.

The cruelty of my family
hurting, maiming,
trying to destroy each other
spread along the tunnel.
My hands shook now

as I froze, every thought
inside my head
was screaming at me
to turn back,
turn back now.

But turning back
meant accepting defeat.
All of this would be for nothing.
I had to continue.
I just had to.

So I took a lavender potion
from my bag of simples
to calm myself,
steeled my nerves
and continued.

The Artist

I did not know what I expected
at the other end of the cave.
But it was not what I found.

At the last crystal there were urns,
purple and red and yellow,
the light shone off the paint

that had carelessly dripped
down these urns like honey.
And there, under the glowing light

was a man with a long dark beard
and wild eyes the colour of the night.
He was on his knees, painting,

wild slashes of his brush
and hands that were old,
yet still strong.

But there was something
about his presence,
a pride mixed with a strange fury.

I hesitated for the briefest of seconds
but it was too late to run.
He had already seen me.

'Who goes there?!'

His deep voice rumbled across the cave,
disturbing the stalactites that hung
from the ceiling. Far behind me,
I heard one fall to the ground.

I was many things, but I was not
a coward of any kind.
So I stepped further into the light,
and said, as strong-voiced as I could,

'My name is Hekate,
Daughter of Asteria and Perses.
And I am trying to pass
through to the Halls of Night.'

His wild eyes took me in,
and I saw that his face,
much like his hands, was withered,
old and weary of something.

'Perses.' He stood up
and stepped towards me.
'Now there is a name
I have not heard in a long time.'

I saw a scar on his throat.
The mottled place where
Zeus had sliced his sword
and unleashed his siblings.

Kronos

What happens to a God-King after a war?
Does he flee? Or is he captured?
And if he is captured,
what punishment is fair for a God-King?
And if he is punished, then for how long?

There are questions I never asked,
for I never considered them.
My uncle Pallas did not speak of the war
after I was left in the Underworld
in his and Styx's care.

He named the war a haunting memory.
He did not like to speak of its consequences.
For the first time I wondered
how he and Styx had managed to get
in Zeus' good graces. What had they done?

My uncle especially refused to talk
of the punishment doled out to my father,
his own brother. But it was Kronos' name
that made his neck tighten, his teeth grit
and his loud voice go very quiet.

Kronos led the Titans, my father by his side,
against his children. They lost. We lost.
So now here he was. A mad king,
who once had the whole cosmos in his palm
and now presided over nothing.

Is this the fate of all God-Kings?

'Come, child. Be not afraid'

There was a desperation in his voice,
and something in my blood told me
to obey. This was Kronos' power.
Time and the command over all our divinity.

Even then, diminished and half of himself,
he had not lost his authority. As though
hypnotized, I walked with him despite
all of my misgivings.

He led me further into the cave.
I could see that even though this was
where he lived forever in exile, it was beautiful.
The walls were even, not earthen,

and a warmth filled the cave here.
The crystals shone more brightly,
and richly coloured fabrics did their best
to make this cavern seem homely.

The floors had been turned to
polished marble and reflected the light
of the crystals above, made the place inviting.
An aroma of game rose through the air

and I noticed that in the centre of the room,
a large bubbling cauldron was
cooking. Divinity did not need food,
but it was one of the luxuries we most enjoyed.

My mouth watered and Kronos smiled.

A Disquieting Truth

Somewhere within the recesses
of my mind, my mother's voice
rose like an ocean in warning.

Hekate, she whispered, her moonlit,
musical tones in my ear after so long,
You cannot stay here. It is not safe.

He was just an old God now,
with no powers, I thought to myself,
and he just wanted someone to speak with.

'It must be difficult,' I said softly,
but I did not finish my sentence.
Of course it was difficult.

He had lost his entire realm.
'We are much the same,
you and I,' he sighed,

Then reached over to the ladle
of the pot and stirred.
'We both lost everything in the war.'

It was the first time anyone
had ever said those words to me.
And it was with a jolt I realized,

His words were *true*.

The Ruse

The air of the cave was filled
with the scent of herbs and meat.

Kronos carefully ladled some
of the stew into a wooden bowl.

As he handed it to me,
he fretted, 'I once had bowls

made of the finest silver taken
from the heart of the earth.

Gifts from my mother.'
Of course, his mother, Gaia.

He sighed as he sat with
his own bowl. 'I think,

out of all of us, it is she
who has suffered the most.'

I pictured the kind-faced Gaia,
roots and ivy for hair,

moss-skinned, doe-eyed
watching her children

fight her grandchildren.
My stomach twisted in sympathy.

I looked at Kronos.
'You are not as the stories said.'

He said nothing to this,
just smiled sadly and ate his own food.

I also ate the stew he had prepared,
the meat was tender and flavourful.

'Thank you,' I said when I finished,
'for your hospitality.' I stood up then,

rifling through my bag for nectar.
I imagined I would need all my strength

to walk through the caves of darkness
into the Halls of the Night.

'I must leave,' I said,
not looking up at him,

'I must go to the Halls of Night
before it is discovered I am gone.'

As I found my flask,
I looked up and saw his face.

It was changed, cold, angry.
And it was then I realized

that his kindness had a price.

'You Will Go Nowhere'

It was like his voice had turned to poison.
Where his tone once dripped

with melancholy, it was now ancient,
laced with the razor-edge of cruelty.

I stayed very still, as though an animal,
believing if I did not move,

my predator may not see me.
'But I must leave.' I could hear the panic

in my own voice. Oh how naive
I had been, I should have run

when I saw him. 'Please,'
I pleaded quietly, the flask clutched

between my fingers as though
a talisman of protection.

I felt the cave swim
and expand before my eyes.

'No.' There was pure venom
in his words now. 'Too long

I have been alone in these caves,
no wife or daughter to care for me.

YOU will be my new consort,
and tend to my every need.'

I gasped. 'I am not yet old enough
to even know my own powers!'

Kronos scoffed. 'You do not need powers,
if all you are going to do is serve me.'

My blurred vision could make out
his shape advancing towards me.

Like a wolf about to pounce
onto its prey.

The Spell

I had eaten that game
without question,
without thinking
that he could have
poisoned it.

It was fortunate
that over the years
my experiments with herbs
had given me a tolerance
to most poisons.

And now as my vision swam
three distinct voices
broke through my mind.
What was *in* that game?
I tried to speak.

My words collided
with the other voices.
Why were there other
voices in my head?

Finally I choked out,
my mouth garbled the words
'What have you done to me?!'
His form loomed before me
as he spoke,

'Be grateful, I have simply
set you free to do your duty.'
I stumbled back from him,

terror gripping me,
and ran even as my own body

fought me.

The Labyrinth

Kronos was the God of Time, and what is time but a maze without end? As I tried in my drugged state to escape his cave, it gave way to a labyrinth of caves. Kronos may be a diminished God, but he knew precisely how to use his powers to confuse me. So I did what I had to do, I chose the cave that had appeared closest to me and stumbled towards it. Behind me I could hear that he had turned into his true size and the thud of his footsteps was louder and slower than mine but they covered more ground. I had forgotten that Kronos was also the father of giants, beings of great stature and strength. I ran through cave after cave, stones and sharp-toothed minerals cut at my bare feet, and still I heard him behind me. It felt like my heart would be torn asunder. Oh if only I had drunk the nectar before this happened, it would have fortified me, but now I was breathless and these tunnels seemed endless. Behind me the Titan ran, his unrelenting roar sending chills through my body. Still, I was silver-footed enough to run faster than he could and it put me in the lead, my single winning hand. Finally, *finally,* I reached a crossroads. Three different cave entrances stared at me. Each looked like the other, crystal-lit until suddenly the crystals died. Trembling, I pulled a torch from my bag, hoping to light my own way – a trick that Styx had taught me, a snap and flick and the fire flew from my fingers to the torch, the darkness fleeing from the flames. *Thank you, Styx*, I whispered softly. My fear had a grip on me as I looked at all three routes in turn, hoping this was not just whatever spell he put on the food toying with my head. I could hear Kronos now. He was snorting, and as I turned, I saw his monstrous form in shadow, close behind me, like the form of a Minotaur. But there was no Minotaur here. This labyrinth held something much more dangerous. A once God-King. Perhaps it was the panic then that made me do it. But whatever the spell was that he gave me was as likely a culprit as the ancient stirring in my blood. Every approaching footstep was evoking something in me, the taste of moulding cavern air, the smell of the danger so close behind was so terrifying, I felt like I would break apart. Like pieces of me were pulling apart, my whole body trying to tear itself into portions. Then suddenly, there was a moment of wrenching pain. My vision suddenly cleared . . . and I split into three.

The Three

I stared into two scared faces
that were both precisely mine.
But before any of us could react,
Kronos' form began to fill the cave.

Our thoughts ran together
like a cascading river.
The panic, and then
the clear instruction:

RUN.

The Race

Each of us took a cave.
Each stumbling as we did.
I could feel them,
the other two me's.

We could think linear thoughts,
the same thing occurred to us at once.
We scrambled over rocks
together in the endless caves

and I saw what they saw.
It was the third version of me
that Kronos gave chase to.
She was the slowest of us

even if by just a fraction.
I heard him behind her,
he was closing in!
I willed her to run faster

while I ran faster myself.
His hand reached out
closing around her
NO NO NO NO

In panic, she shoved her torch
into his face and as though
he had seen his own monster
he roared in fear and dropped her

and she scrambled to her feet and . . .

'KRONOS!'

It was the voice of a dozen gorgons,
thunderous with frightening fury.
It was the sound of a hundred sirens,
screaming against the ocean wind.
It was the cry of a thousand harpies,
screeching before they descended on prey.

So primordial was this sound
that the three I had split into
were jarred back together as one.
The raging pain pulsed through
my whole body as I felt the other
two versions of me stitch themselves

back into my body again,
and I felt myself burn and stretch
and return until there were
no others like me left.
Only one.
Just me.

And then the voice
filled the whole room again.
'REMEMBER, TITAN,
WHERE YOU STAND.
YOUR OATH TO ME AND HADES
DEMANDS AN ANSWER.'

Kronos, who had been terrifying
to me, suddenly sounded very small.
'F-forgive me, Goddess of the Dark.
I . . . I have simply been lonely.'

There was a terrible, cold silence
that followed and then the voice spoke.

'LET THIS BE THE LAST TIME
YOU BREAK YOUR OATH,
FOR THE NEXT TIME,
IT IS TARTARUS
OR STYX'S WATER.
THE CHOICE IS YOURS.'

I could hear the warble in his voice
as he whispered, 'I apologize.
I am so sorry.' A shaking sob
escaped his chest.
And that was when the voice
turned its attentions to me.

'HEKATE, CHILD OF ASTERIA
AND PERSES. YOU WILL BE
BROUGHT TO THE HALLS
OF NIGHT WHERE YOU WILL
EXPLAIN YOUR PURPOSE
FOR THIS INTRUSION.'

I winced at the word *intrusion*.
But before I could acknowledge
the message, a hurricane of darkness
swept me off my feet,
turning everything around me
into a swirling abyss.

The Goddess of the Night

It was as though a black river had attached itself to every pore of my skin. It was unforgiving and hot and I hated it as I struggled to breathe through it. Fortunately the feeling did not last long as I was left on a smooth, cool floor, gasping in the musty air. Like a sentient being rather than fog, the black river seeped away as if it had been dismissed. As my eyes cleared from the dark abyss, I saw where I was. This room was shaped like a dome. Around it a hundred altars smoked with prayers from distant mortals far away. It seemed like there were no windows here at first glance, but I realized that the giant arched windows did exist as the glitter of thousands of stars gleamed through them. A throne made from a million diamonds shone from the centre of the room. And on this throne, her head adorned with a coronet carved from the glowing heart of a dying star, sat the Goddess of the Night, Nyx. Her face was youthful but her eyes were ancient, a glinting pair of onyxes the colour of her skin. It did not take a second glance to determine what I already knew. She was *furious*. Perhaps the rumours were just rumours. Perhaps Goddesses were as unwelcome as Gods were here. And I was not even a Goddess. Just the child of two forgotten Gods.

'COME HERE, CHILD'

Her voice was softer than it was
in Kronos' cave, but I could still hear
every monster of the night it hid inside.

I shuddered, a cold in my veins.
I knew she did not like uninvited guests
inside her realm, and I had disobeyed.

Slowly, I stood on my own two feet,
and began to walk towards her, inch by inch.
I summoned all my courage.

But as I was walking,
I saw him, the dark-robed
figure with a kind face at her side.

It struck me in this moment
that this was the boy
who helped me with Cerberus.

But what was he doing here?
Why would he be
in Nyx's realm?

It was his scythe
that gave him away.
Her favourite son.

Thanatos,
the God of Peaceful
Death and Endings.

Our Eyes Met

And recognition seized us both.
He was older now,
his face had grown more defined.
He no longer had the boyish youth
I had seen in him.

His cheekbones sat high
and though his hair was shorn,
it only did more to emphasize
his finely cut features
that seemed tenderly carved

from the loving hands
of an ancient being.
He was beautiful in a way
I had never seen before
and I felt the pull again.

Closer to the throne,
I realized his tired eyes
were rich with promise,
and a soft charcoal
the shades of grey of a storm.

I saw his lips upturn slightly
as I approached the throne,
and his smile gave me
a comfort I did not realize
I needed.

At Nyx's Throne

Nyx was my great-aunt.
My grandmother Gaia
was her sister; they both
came from the womb of Chaos,
the creator of the universe.

They were the oldest of our family.
All Gods were somehow
aunts, uncles, cousins
brothers and sisters
to each other.

But what was different
about Nyx was that she
inspired a kind of fear
from other Gods simply
through the mention of her name.

It is said that even Zeus
knew better than to enter
her domain without permission
and here I was,
not even a Goddess,

standing at the base of
her throne. She did not move,
her onyx eyes set upon me
with a primeval anger.
Then she spoke coldly,

'YOU MUST RETURN
TO YOUR GUARDIANS
IMMEDIATELY.'

I do not know
what came over me,
but I looked into her eyes,
my chin raised stubbornly,
my feet planted firmly,
and spoke loud and clearly.

'NO.'

The Dark Fog Returned

I saw it swirl from around her chair,
filling the floors of the room.
I could feel its moist constraints
at my ankles. It looked like
a wine-dark ocean, rich with danger.

This was a threat.

I knew it as I saw it.
She leaned forward,
her dark dress of diamond stars
turning into rubies as she kept
her eyes on mine.

'CHILD. DO YOU NOT KNOW
TO WHOM YOU SPEAK?'

Now or Never

I told myself, as the night sky outside
filled with an obsidian storm.

Standing as tall as I could, I met
the Night Goddess' eyes and spoke.

'When you were young, Goddess,
Chaos gave you your name, your gifts,

and even your curses. You knew
your story and your destiny

because your mother had dreams
and she was able to give them to you.'

My voice quivered slightly. 'Neither
my mother nor my father could do this for me.

All I want to know is my divine purpose.
The Fates hold that answer. I am sure of it.

Do you not believe that divine blood
should know what their immortality is for?'

I watched her face as a series
of nameless expressions crossed it.

But before she could speak—

'I Will Take Her, Mother'

His voice was soft and gentle.
It had to be. Thanatos was the God
of bringing peace in death.

I could see his storm-dark eyes clearer now,
so like his mother's, but kinder.
And much more tired.

His mouth looked quicker
to smile than to frown
and that told me everything.

As the hurricane outside died,
and the dark fog melted away,
Thanatos stepped forward,

laying his scythe down at
his mother's feet, a gesture of respect.
'She too is the child of Gods,

just like you and me.
I will take her to the Fates
for the knowledge she craves.'

Nyx tapped the arm of her throne,
her expression adrift now
in a thousand thoughts.

I thought I knew how slowly
time, that old trickster, could move
when I was alone on Styx's riverbanks.

But nothing seemed longer
than waiting for Nyx
to make up her mind.

I saw her face harden,
and steeled myself for a refusal.
But then she looked at Thanatos

and grudgingly,
to my surprise,
she nodded in agreement.

Thanatos

If I had not met him here, I wonder if I would know him to be the God of Peaceful Death. His face was warm as a tree bark in summer, even if his eyes were as ancient as the earth bed itself. He was quick to grasp his scythe and lead me out the halls. His gait was slower than Hermes', who held a spring in his step wherever he went. Thanatos was a much older God than Hermes or even Hades — even though his features spoke of a strange, ageless youth. It had been his scythe that had given so many a quiet dreamless sleep even when they were gasping in pain. In the fields of Asphodel everyone spoke of him as the Kind One, how he had visited battlefields to end soldiers' pain. How it was such a relief to give themselves over to his tender voice, sometimes after a lifetime of agony. Perhaps then it was in his nature to care for lost souls seeking relief from pain. Whether those lost souls were mortals . . . or Gods. We crossed through the Realm of Night, the birthplace of every single night that blessed the mortal world. Here midnight came to life, a cloak of royal blue soil and a wealth of deep purple and grey skies that looked like a bruise. It was beautiful in its own way, rich with dusky rivers and silver flowers. In the bruised sky, a shimmer of stars and two separate moons lit our way, one bougainvillea pink and one ocean blue. Finally, Thanatos stopped and I peeked around him to see why but had to shut my eyes to the brightness before me. A river flowed but it was a strange river, bright with gemstones every colour you could possibly imagine and more. This was the river of memory.

Mnemosyne

Before she was a river,
Mnemosyne was a Goddess
seeking her own voice
in an ever-changing world.

One of Gaia's golden children,
she knew she held command
over the domain of memory,
the gift of remembrance.

But what good is a power
if no one teaches you how to use it?
After the Titanomachy
she set out to find answers.

Along the way she met a shepherd
who promised to help her.
For nine days and nine nights
they spoke of the stars

and the beauty of truths,
but on the very end of the ninth day,
this shepherd revealed
he had tricked her,

for he was truly
the God-King Zeus.
The story could end there,
but Mnemosyne was an ancient Goddess,

and in her womb she carried
her vengeance.

Nine Goddesses were born
of her. Each one

holding power over every art
and every craft beloved to the Gods.
And with her gift of memory,
she ensured that Zeus remembered

if he ever crossed her again,
she would empty his world
of everything beautiful,
fill his mind with only that

which caused pain.
In an effort to amend
his brother's grave errors,
Hades gave her safety

in the form of this river
and sway over the realm
of memory. It was her waters
that gave us the gift of remembering.

Crossing Mnemosyne

Thanatos drew me to a battered boat
tied to a dock at the bank of the river.

'It is safe,' he told me,
seeing the hesitance in my features.

To demonstrate, he stepped in first,
and gestured with his scythe for me to get in.

I followed his movements
and stepped into the vessel.

A soft sprinkling could be heard
as the gems scratched at the sides

of the little boat. But it appeared to be
made of good strong oak so it resisted.

I stared at the gems as they moved.
It was like they were floating.

'Those are memories.' Thanatos' voice
seeped into my thoughts. He twisted his scythe

and the wood twisted to become
a long paddle, which he dipped into

the gemstones. The boat
moved uneasily through the current.

'What you did took courage.'

'What Took Courage?' I Asked Him

'Your audacity with Nyx.'
It surprised me that he did not refer to
the Goddess of the Night as his mother.
'Not many have had the courage—'

'And remain to tell the tale?'
I finished his sentence. It struck me
in that moment that it was true.
Nyx left no one unscathed when pushed.

'What is it like,' I asked him,
'to have her as your mother?'
The corners of his mouth lifted,
and his brow raised slightly with mirth.

'She is as loving as she is terrifying.'
I would have asked what he meant,
but he was pulling into the bay.
Beyond us lay a legend

from which only few came back whole.

The Forest of Silence

When people ask about the dominion of Hades, very few speak about the Forest of Silence. It was a dark mimicry of a mortal forest, as though a cruel God had decided to make a mockery of everything we loved about them. With its trees that had roots and bark made of vipers, and carnivorous black rabbits and poisonous midnight deer that would chase you until you fell to them, this was not a place many entered willingly. Everything here thirsted for blood and ichor; the trees would try to drink from you while crushing your bones into dust. There were stories, of course. Tales of things that knew how to tear you apart and piece you back together, the forest becoming a maze that never let you out. A thousand monsters were born here every day: they said that Echidna, mother of monsters, had hidden her womb somewhere in this forest, ensuring a constant stream of progeny. The screams and screeches reminded me of my visit to Tartarus. My stomach clenched with worry each time I heard an otherworldly sound. But as I looked upon the dark foreboding of the woods, all I could see was the hope that lay on the other side. And that was enough to make my feet move.

Thanatos Knew These Woods So Well

It quelled my fears. I wondered if the folktales told by the mortals in Asphodel about him and his siblings were true: that they grew up with monster playmates instead of Godlings; whether this forest was where they played their games. It struck me then how he had grown up with monsters for companions and I had had my ghosts, our childhoods intertwined with their strangeness. Perhaps this was why he had been so tender with Cerberus? He knew how to be gentle with monsters, just like I had a love for my spirits that no one else understood. I had so much I wanted to ask him, but Thanatos walked these woods in complete silence. Whether this was because he was trying to avoid the attention of what lived here or he simply enjoyed the quiet, I did not know. What I did know was that at one point, a scaled darkness wrapped around my leg and with a single swipe of his scythe it was cut in two, leaving red sap across my skin. Shuddering, I wiped it off. We could have been walking for hours or days. We did not stop, though the tiredness of this quest was starting to wear on my bones. But I held my tongue, and I was glad for it, because soon we saw it: the impossibly tall black towers of Hades' palace.

Hades' Domain

Thanatos was watching me
as we emerged from the woods,
brambles stuck in our clothes
and blue-black leaves caught
in our hair. I took in the
four strange obsidian towers
that simply disappeared
into the earth's crust above us

and the skulls that had been
hammered into the walls
as though a morbid decoration.
Bats flew everywhere,
one even landed in my hair,
but I shook it out before it settled.
Thanatos gestured to a small archway
at the very back of the palace.

It was twice his height
and I began to walk towards it,
but then he said, 'We will take this way;
it is the servants' door.'
With two thumps from
his scythe, the heavy doors
swung open. He walked ahead of me
whispering, 'Be very quiet,
and let me do all of the talking.'

I Sensed It Before I Saw It

The thing that protected these halls.
It was less of a presence and more
of a feeling. A fear and then
a hollowing of your spirit.

It liked to toy with its prey
before it appeared, or so
I had heard. When it had fed
enough on my dread,

a hooded creature with long robes,
clawed hands that hung
with decayed flesh,
appeared before us.

Red eyes glowing
like ominous lanterns
in its hood.
This was a God in Grey.

And it stood
massive and unforgiving before us.
Thanatos cleared his throat.
'Let us pass. We are here to see the Fates.'

It lifted its huge monster claw
and pointed at me. 'She should not
be here,' it whispered in an old, unused voice.
'She is here with me.' Thanatos was quiet,

but his voice was forceful. The thing did not move.
'You can pass, but leave her here with me.'

I did not want to be left here.
Not with this thing.

Thanatos shook his head,
'I am on a duty for Nyx.'
The creature let out a rasp and I realized
it was laughing. 'Your mother

has no sway in Hades' halls,
Godling. Give the child to me.'
I froze, my eyes wide.
Thanatos and I had just met properly.

He had no reason to fight for me,
especially at great risk to himself.
I took a step back, cursing
my own naivety, and the creature

advanced towards me.
But Thanatos raised his scythe
and blocked its way.
'Do not go any closer to her.'

The words were soft,
but even I recognized
the cold edges of danger,
a challenge, threatened fury.

Eager to dispel the situation,
I wracked my brains
as the God in Grey growled,
and then I remembered it:

the golden apple I stole
from Elysium. It was still

inside my bag of simples.
Even Gods weren't meant to eat it.

I knew these creatures loved Hades' orchards.
Perhaps it was because of the fruit?
'Wait! I have come with offerings!'
I said, opening my satchel and removing

the golden apple, 'A gift for you.
And in return, please let us through.'
The creature glared down
at the offering in my hands.

For a moment, the air felt
suffocating as Thanatos and I
waited to see what this terrifying
being would do.

Finally, I felt the air clear
as my trick worked,
and the thing snatched
the apple from my hand,

slowly moving to give us way.
Thanatos looked at me
as we walked past
the strange beast-God.

'Did you steal that from
the Hesperides?' he asked,
and I could hear the laughter
tucked in the corners of his question.

He was referring to his four sisters,
named after the setting colours of the sun,

who guarded a garden full
of golden apples with untold secrets.

I decided I liked the sound
of his amusement.
'Promise me you will not tell Hermes.
I stole it from the Elysian Fields.'

And this made his amusement
turn into a deep, warm laugh.

Hades' Throne Room

Every throne room in this palace
spoke of the blood after which
they were created.

Hades' throne room
was no different. Like him,
it was not opulent.

The only soft furnishing
was the black carpet
that led up to the throne

made of skeletons
and old bones dipped
in molten hematite so they shone.

The austerity made them stand out,
the three Goddesses in gold.
One maiden, one mother, one crone.

They sat at the foot of the throne,
a giant loom before them
that spun golden thread

as they sang to it.
I took in a sharp breath
as I recognized her.

The old woman
from the Asphodel Meadows
who gave me a tale.

Courage

I told myself
as Thanatos gently
nudged me forward
with his scythe.

Courage

I whispered to my feet
as they walked to
the giant loom
and all of its spun gold.

Courage

I thought as the crone
saw my face
with a spark
of recognition.

Courage

I implored
as she slowly
treaded towards me,
a smile across her face.

'Please . . . '

I was so eager,
I did not even know
what to ask her.

And then the crone spoke,
her smile never wavering.
'The answer you seek is not here.'

At first I thought
I had misheard her.
'But you must know my purpose!

And I found something
along the journey,'
I was speaking quickly now.

'I became three!
Three versions of myself.
Like you!'

I gestured towards the mother
and maiden who were looking
closely at me now.

I turned back to the crone,
'How did I become three?
You must know something,

you know the fates
of everyone,
mortal or God!'

'The Answer You Seek Is Not Here'

It was like every wound
I ever had opened up
inside my chest and I wanted to weep.

It was like seeing my home crumble
and losing my mother all over again.
Like someone I trusted shoved a knife

into my belly, and although my divinity
would not let me die, I felt as close to
death as I had ever been.

My voice was high and shaking
as I said to her, 'Please, I have
travelled such a long way here.'

You must give me something.
The unspoken words suspended between us,
soft and pleading and desperate.

The crone simply smiled,
every wrinkle on her face creasing.
'And that journey was not in vain,

child. Even in barren ground
there are flowers that find a way
to grow. But this is not the place

in which you will find what you seek.'

Disappointment

Gods do not know what to do with loss.
It is so rare for us to lose things
that when it does happen,
we use our powers to destroy entire lands.

But I was a Goddess with no gifts,
just a hollow emptiness
and a dry mouth that watched
as the crone returned to her loom.

She never once looked to me again.
Stifling a sob, I turned and ran past Thanatos.
Past the God in Grey
who was a sitting in a gibbering heap,

the half-eaten apple clutched tight
in its cold hand. Past the red-hued
obsidian halls of Hades' unforgiving,
cold palace. All the way to the edge

of the Forest of Silence, where the scale
of unknown dangers and the snake-headed roots
made me stop. Finally,
I fell to my knees and sobbed.

'I'm Sorry'

I was so deep within the moors of my grief
I had not heard Thanatos approach.
Even though the forest was a vacuum
of such deep silence that even a twig
cracking far enough away was amplified
till it echoed within your head.
I turned at his words, and saw
he had removed his hood.

His hair was dark like his mother's,
but shorn close to his scalp.
He rubbed his head slightly,
almost an uneasy action,
and then said again,
'I am sorry you did not find
the answers you need.'
I stifled another sob out of pride

at his words and looked up at him.
'I will survive.' The words were colder
than I intended them to be,
but he nodded without flinching
at my tone. For some time
we sat there in silence,
the shrieks and sounds
of the forest beyond softening
into my haze of grief.

'I do not know what to do,'
I said quietly, more to myself
than to him. 'How am I to learn
my own gifts if no one will help me?'
Thanatos looked thoughtfully at me,

then crouched down next
to where I had collapsed and
lifted my chin with a gentle hand.
'I have watched you from afar
for a long time, Hekate.'

His words made my stomach flutter,
the touch of his fingers tender.
'Pallas forbade any of us other
than Charon from speaking to you.
So I watched you from a distance,
apart from that one time you were
with Cerberus.'
I frowned at this. 'But why?'
He hesitated with his answer,
then stopped and rose.

It hung in the air, my question.
There are secrets Pallas
does not want me to know,
I realized with a jolt.
But Thanatos was not done.
He stood and gave me his hand.
I took it in mine and rose to my feet.
He looked lost in thought,
then his face cleared
and after some contemplation he said,

'Accompany me
on my duties.'

I don't know what made me agree.
This was an odd request.

And yet, I asked no questions.
And yet, I simply said, 'Yes.'

The Land of the Living

What shocked me out of my grief
was just how simple it was
to find our way out of Hades.

In my still-young mind
I had thought it would be
the current of a thousand seas,

the might of a hundred furies,
a path divined to be so long
that the traveller gave up

and simply returned to the Underworld.
Instead, Thanatos took the boat
to the very end of Mnemosyne

and together we walked out
of the Cave of Dusk, just as
Helios rode his chariot to set

the glorious gold of the sun.
The outside of the cave was drenched
in a better gold than the Elysian Fields.

Every flower, every blade of grass
would live a shorter life, but
as the warm earth beneath my feet

told me, this was the way
it was supposed to be
in the land of the living.

The Duties of Death

I.

The first home we visited smelled of disease. I should not have known this smell, but the decayed, bitter air made me cough. In the very first room, an old woman lay on a cot surrounded by her two sons, their wives and seven children. She was frail, her paper-thin hands shook upon the sheets. Thanatos, unseen by the family, walked towards her. He took her hand and when her tired face, pale-lipped, turned towards him, he smiled and nodded. With a sigh of relief, the woman looked back and took a long, shuddering last breath. Thanatos reached forward and closed her eyes gently. As the family realized she was gone and the sons wept, Thanatos released her hands into theirs and the silver spirit of the woman rose. 'Thank you,' she whispered softly, and he nodded. With two quick movements of his scythe, her spirit disappeared.

It was here that I learned that death was the gentle art of release.

II.

The second place we stopped at was not a home but a tree. I watched Thanatos climb this tree with an ease I did not expect someone with such cumbersome robes to do, but perhaps he was used to it by now. It was a graceful oak, its bark ringed with its age. I watched him move something from the branches and then move down as swiftly as he had climbed up. From his pocket he produced three small silver spirits – a trio of baby birds, still so tiny that they could not possibly fly. I looked at him in shock. What could have killed them up in their nest? And then it struck me, looking at their emaciated bodies. Their mother had not returned in some time. So they had starved. Later, Thanatos would tell me that the mother had been killed by a hawk.

This taught me how one death could be the reason behind more. That mortality was frequently dependent on other mortal life.

III.

Thanatos led me through a village decorated with fresh irises and white flowers. Spring had brought her bounty here. Everything looked like the aftermath of a celebration, overturned urns once filled with wine, leftover grapes and bones being chewed on by the village dogs. But it was only when I saw the shells and peacock feathers, an altar smoking with jasmine and myrrh, that I realized that this was a wedding. I turned wide-eyed to Thanatos, who looked straight ahead and walked into the pale-blue, walled house at the centre of the village. When they told the story later, it was that a serpent crept through the night and killed the sleeping groom.

I learned in those dark moments, as Thanatos walked back with the groom, that there are only so many breaths to a mortal life. And that death, though unfair, is a great equalizer.

This knowledge did not stop me from weeping for the new bride, still dreaming of a future that was kind and full.

The Island

It was past dawn
when Thanatos told me
that we were going to collect
the final soul of this day.

We were on an island,
a harsh, rock-strewn place full
of sheep and coarse land
and the heat of the morning sun

already beating down on a golden beach
where a little boy sat alone.
My mouth tasted ash.
Was this the final soul?

As we moved closer, I saw
that the boy was cradling
something in his arms,
burning sobs racking his body.

I realized that the thing
in the boy's arms
was a small pup,
breathing his last.

A Boy and His Dog

The boy looked up at us
and I saw the devastation
that leaked from his sorrow-filled eyes.

He lifted the bundle towards us.
'Please can you help him?
He is my only friend.'

My heart clutched at his words.
I knew what it was like to have
familiar love taken from you.

I turned to Thanatos,
who simply shook his head.
Of course, this was death's duty.

But I had to help this boy,
even if it was just a kind word.
So I knelt into the hot sand

and reached for the small animal.
'I am so sorry,' I whispered,
as he drew his final breath.

My hand felt him go still.
The boy's sobs turned into a wail.
But then, just as his heart broke . . .

A spark inside the animal grew
till it began to glow red and gold.
The pup took a deep breath
and as though the last moments

had not even happened,
he leapt out of the boy's arms

into mine and began
to lick my face.
I sat there, shocked,

as the boy whooped with joy,
picking the little dog up
and holding him tight.

'Careful,' I heard Thanatos say.
'You do not want to squeeze
the life he just got back out of him.'

The boy nodded and set
the wriggling pup on the ground
where he ran circles around us.

Thanatos smiled and knelt
so the pup could rush towards him.
The boy took my hands and kissed them.

'Lady Goddess, thank you,
thank you, thank you
for bringing Argos back to me!'

I numbly shook my head,
'No . . . I am no Goddess. I did nothing.'
I felt Thanatos' hand on my shoulder.

'Hekate, you did.
You brought that animal
back to life.'

The boy beamed. 'Goddess Hekate,
when I am King of Ithaca,
we will raise a statue in your name.'

I managed a smile,
I could not imagine
what he possibly meant,

but he had called me Goddess.
'Thank you,' I whispered,
unable to think of anything else.

'And what is your name?'
My voice wobbled this out.
The pup was now racing

around us barking playfully.
It wanted to go
and play, it seemed.

The boy stood up
and gently helped me to my feet.
'My name is Prince Odysseus
and this is my dog Argos.'

Years from now, the poets
won't tell this story.
But Odysseus' name will be
as immortal as any God's.

The Return

I was still trying to understand
what I had managed to do
when I realized that Thanatos
had brought me back to my palace.

This palace, which had never
quite felt like home, but now
the marble corridors
were strangers to me.

Even the kitchen table
I loved seemed like a novelty
from a time barely remembered.
And there, sitting at the table,

her split eyes
filled with more fury
than I had ever seen,
was Styx.

Styx's Rage

'Where,' she spoke slowly,
iciness dripping from her voice,
'have you been?'

I felt Thanatos' presence by my side.
'She was with me.' His voice was firm,
scythe on the floor.

'I had to know, Aunt,' I said softly.
Thanatos' calm company helped.
There was a long, pregnant pause,

as the Goddess who had taken me in
stood up slowly, her snarl
showing her fangs.

'What you did not know
was protecting you, foolish child!'
And then she glared at Thanatos.

'And you, this was your doing?
Do all of the Night's children
think they are above and beyond

consequence—'
'She would have found out one day,'
Thanatos interrupted calmly. 'It should

be with someone who cares for her.'
At this I stilled as though slapped.
'You . . . both knew?'

The Truth

It was the first time
I had seen her
like *this*.

Her anger was still there,
but her face flitted between fury
and something else.

Later I would learn,
that was called guilt.
And what would make
the river of hatred feel guilty?

This is the answer:
she knew what I was,
and she *did not tell me*.

I took a deep breath.

'How Could You Hide This From Me?'

My voice was so small and broken,
I barely recognized it as my own.

'We were trying to protect you,'
Styx whispered softly.

'It's true, Hekate.'
My uncle Pallas' voice filled the room.

He had been watching
from the doorway all this time.

He glared at Thanatos.
'I thought I told you to stay away.'

A controlled anger I had never seen
reverberated off him.

But the God of Death shook his head.
'She needed help you were

refusing to give her, Pallas.'
His voice was so calm compared to theirs.

Pallas' whole body was rigid now.
'And you thought that *you* were the answer.'

'I am simply not arrogant enough to believe
Hekate does not know what is best for herself,'

Thanatos retorted evenly.

My uncle frowned at his words
and turned to me.

'How do you think
the Olympians would take it

if they learned you can undo
all of the Gods' work

by a simple touch of your hand?'
My mind swam at this,

'I . . . I do not understand.'
Thanatos gently reached for my hand.

'Let me explain,' he said softly,
casting a wary eye at my aunt and uncle.

'The Gods rely on mortals dying.
Fear makes those mortals pray.

Those prayers make the Gods
they worship strong,

and the Gods they pray to most
are the ruling Gods on Olympus.'

The pieces began to fall into place.
And then Styx added,

'Now imagine if Zeus found out
that a child of Titans had your

kind of power.' Her voice dropped
to a soft whisper as though

even the walls of the palace
were listening, 'What would happen

to you if they found out you
were a necromancer?'

So that is what I was.
Necromancer.

I Began to Understand

Styx refusing to allow me to talk
to the dead or other immortals.

Pallas forbidding Thanatos
from speaking to me.

The way the boy's dog
rose to life at my touch.

Why I loved the mortal dead
in the Asphodel Fields with their stories.

Pallas was speaking softly now,
his voice distant in my haze.

'The capacity to bring the dead
back to life is something even Hades

does not possess, and neither does
Thanatos, who is death itself.

If Zeus found out . . .'
He did not finish his sentence.

'This is why we had to keep it,
and you, a secret,' said Styx softly.

She reached for me but I stepped back.
They had lied to me.

I stared at them.
'Is there more?'

They exchanged a look
and hesitated.

'There is,' I breathed.
'You will tell me now,' I demanded.

'Tell Her, River Goddess'

I turned to see Charon glowering
at both my uncle and aunt.

No one had heard him arrive
but there he stood, storm-eyed.

'I warned you she would find out.'
His words had a hard edge to them

that I had never heard before.
'Tell her, or I will.'

Pallas took a warning step towards
Charon. 'This is a matter for family—'

Thanatos shook his head.
'You know we are all family.'

It was true. Thanatos and Charon
were brothers, sons of Nyx.

Titans too, just like me, Styx and Pallas.
The same wretched, broken

family that kept secrets, lied
and warred with each other.

I was shaking with anger.
'Your father, Hekate—' started Charon,

but Pallas stopped him.
'I will tell her,' he growled.

Then he looked at me. 'Your father,
Hekate, was my brother.

We grew up together
and he was my dearest friend.

So when the war came,
Of course I chose his side.

But then . . . we were losing . . .
and Styx and I had four young children.'

He hesitated and looked at Styx.
My stomach clenched.

'Styx went to Asteria.
They shared a childhood, and were

dear to each other once. She asked her,
begged her to talk to your father.

If he had surrendered,
his punishment would not have been

quite so harsh. But your mother
refused to listen. So . . . we . . .

We had no choice left.
We had to turn to Zeus.'

The sickness of these words
spread like ivy through my mind.

'You . . . you *both* betrayed my parents?
For *Zeus and the Olympians?!*'

Styx had betrayed my mother.
Styx had betrayed my mother.

All this time I thought it was just Pallas,
but no. It was Styx too.

No wonder this palace never felt
as though it was home.

It was built of guilt and betrayals
so large they could not be forgiven.

Styx called my name and stepped
around the table towards me

but I stumbled back from her
and *ran*.

It Hurt It Hurt *It Hurt*

like a thousand knives in my skin.
Styx and Pallas had both betrayed my parents,

and they had lied to me.
They would not even tell me

what my godhood was for
and they intended to keep it

a secret forever.
I took in a deep, shuddering breath

when I was outside,
and I let myself crumble to the earth.

I heard Thanatos
and Charon following me,

Pallas and Styx shouting
for me to wait,

but before they could reach me
I opened my mouth wide

and screamed and screamed
until I split in three again.

At the Crossroads Again

It felt like this splitting
was connected to the many
crossroads of my life.
I could not stop when it happened,
the pain of being split physically
reflected the pain of splitting within
and the three of us screamed together,
bodies stiff in the agony
of what was discovered,
and when we stopped,
when we *had* to stop
because our throats
were so sore that the screams
were nothing more than croaks,
we sobbed and sobbed until
finally I felt a hand on my shoulder.

'Hekate.' The whisper was so soft
I knew it had to be Thanatos.
I looked up into his kind eyes,
the same eyes that had recognized me
in his mother's halls
and then aided me on my journey.
The same eyes that had watched
me break after the crone's words
in Hades' throne room
and I realized how much
I needed the truth. Charon stood
beside his brother, his face
marred with worry. I trusted
no one but them now.
But there was something else.
Their gaze was fixed

on something behind me.
I followed it to the direction
of the palace door.

Except there was no door left.
There was only Styx and Pallas
staring at a pile of rubble,
which was the palace they had
built for me. I had done that.
My screaming had done that.
I felt a sharp crack on both sides
of my spine and knew that
the other two versions of me
had abandoned me too.

The End of Something

Styx stepped forward
but I raised a hand to stop her.
'No.' A word laced with pain.

'Please, let us explain,'
Pallas tried now,
but I shook my head.

'You had years to explain.
There is nothing left
for you to say.'

Styx's eyes
were agonized.
'But where will you go?'

I felt the warmth
of Thanatos' hand
take mine.

'She will go with me.'
I turned to him
and he smiled reassuringly.

'I will build my own home,'
I said, but Thanatos spoke.
'I will help you.'

There was such a gentleness
to his words. *You will not
have to do this alone.*

Charon put a comforting
hand on my shoulder.
'And I will aid too.'

Friendship. Kindness.
I did not need rescuing,
but I did need those.

'You cannot do this.'
Styx's voice broke.
'I made a promise, Hekate.'

I shook my head.
'You made that promise
to my mother. Not to me.'

This schism between us
was only widening now
and for a time that felt

like a thousand years
during which none of us spoke.
Then I said to Thanatos

and to Charon,
'We must leave.'
And we did.

From the rubble
and ashes of the life
I used to know.

A WOMAN OF POWER

PART THREE

Womanhood

Pallas had once asked Styx, when he thought I was not listening, whether I would ever become a woman. It may have occurred to them that perhaps keeping my abilities from me was stopping me from becoming the Goddess I was meant to be. I felt as though I had been trapped as a girl for a century. But the moment I left the rubble of the palace Styx and Pallas had built me and Thanatos asked me where I wanted my new home to be, I knew. It would be at the banks of Mnemosyne. Close to the Realm of Night, but not quite within Nyx's territory. Close to Thanatos' own palace, but not too close to him either. Easy enough for Charon to reach, but far enough that I would have my solitude to work on the gifts of my godhood. Thanatos told me on our journey there that the love I had of mixing herbs and potions was actually another facet of my power. He called it *mageia*. Magic. And he said I was either a *pharmakis*, a maker of potions, or an *aoidos*, an enchantress. Too little was known of *mageia*; among the Gods, only my mother knew how to practise it. This practice too was a threat to the order of the Gods. I was starting to feel as though my entire existence was a threat. Perhaps this was what womanhood was. The dangerous knowledge of who you are and what you could do with that power if pushed.

A New Body and Home

I would not have noticed it,
I was so busy building
my own palace on the shore
of Mnemosyne, collecting bones
and crystal-like memories

to make way for my new home.
It simply happened that one day
I was standing next to Thanatos
as we built my palace
and then I realized,

he no longer towered over me.
Instead, we stood almost
shoulder to shoulder,
willing the white marble
to settle into the earth's crust.

A grand wooden kitchen
full of everlasting food.
A white marble and
obsidian hall to greet guests
and play dice.

But my favoured room,
the one I loved most,
was in the onyx tower
that rose through the earth's crust
into the land of the living.

Hidden from mortal eyes
by a forest, it was there
that I had built a home

for the owls I would take in
as my very own.

Charon helped carve
heavy oaken doors
for me. And often,
we would all sit on
the banks of Mnemosyne.

It was the most at peace
I had felt since
I had been in
my first home
with my mother.

A Series of Things I Had Learned

I.

When I was young, the halls of Olympus were full of laughter from Zeus and his family, laughter at Titans like me, for what are we but diminished Gods relegated to half of what we used to have. So many of us Titans lost our powers to the Olympians after the war and those that did not end up like my father and mother, were drained of everything that brought them their godhood.

II.

My ability to split into three in times of chaos and pain meant that I was destined to be the Goddess of Crossroads and guide lost travellers to their destination. It was Hermes who taught me this one day, when he showed me that, like him, I was a divinity who ruled boundaries. We sometimes crafted liminal spaces together – where the boundaries of death and life were blurred like in dreams – but I lacked his cruel streak and his acerbic cleverness. What I once thought was beautiful about him was now a thing that made me cautious of him.

III.

I missed Styx. I missed Pallas. I had not spoken to them since the day I walked away, but this did not mean I did not watch them from a distance. Their younger children were grown and visited them now. I watched my cousins from afar. Like their parents, the four of them represented brutal, beautiful things: Zelus, the God of Zeal; Nike, the Goddess of Victory; Kratos, the God of Strength; and Bia, the Goddess of Force. They walked together on the banks of their mother's river, just like I used to as a child. Sometimes, they challenged each other to playful fights. They were skilled warriors and often drew ichor from each other but later laughed about it. There was a cruelty that sharpened each of their features but paradoxically, it suited them.

It was who they were. They were chthonic children, made of dirt and untold things, just like me.

IV.

Charon and Thanatos were the only two friends who had remained with me through all of it – but then, they were the only two friends I had ever made in this Underworld. They had been with me from the naming of all my gifts, while I learned how they worked, and of the dark power that lay within them. In my new home, they stood together stoic, watching me as I practised my art over corpses – every failure to raise the dead, every time I succeeded.

V.

I knew how to make stopped hearts beat again, how to make blood run back through veins, how to raise a dead mortal back into life, but still there was no way for me to bring my mother back or release my father from his fate. What use was it to be this powerful without the ability to help those I love? Even with all this power, I still had to navigate two worlds. One with the rules of Hades, which held my father captive. The other with the rules of Olympians, which determined that I could not bring back my mother. The more my powers grew, the more frustrated I became with these divine rules, which felt like a golden cage designed to keep Goddesses in our place. What use was it to have all these gifts if I could not have what I wanted – my parents finally free? The three of us together, as a family.

VI.

Olympus knew. And the sound that swelled from their halls around my name was not laughter. But hushed whispers of fear.

Thanatos

It was past twilight,
my favoured time of day.
The moon was already glowing.
I was up in my onyx tower,
feeding an injured white owl

that had found its way to me.
As I brushed the ointment
on the underside of its wing,
I heard a voice behind me.
'That one will live long.'

I turned to see Thanatos
at the top of the stairwell.
He wore his usual cloak,
his scythe by his side
and had the same tired, kind eyes,

but there was something
different about him.
I must have been staring
too long because he asked,
'Have I got bone dust on my face?'

I laughed at his question
and shook my head,
'No. Your face is perfect.'
There was a pause as we
both realized what I had said.

'What I mean is . . . ' I fumbled
for words to cover
my stumble, 'I meant . . . '

Thanatos' eyes shone
with mirth as he responded.

'I know what you meant.'
He gestured to the owl
watching us in annoyance.
'If you are finished helping
your friend there, perhaps

you would like to join me
for a meal?' My cheeks burned,
and the owl hooted impatiently at me.
I turned to begin bandaging
its wing and when I was done,

it hopped onto its perch.
I turned back to Thanatos,
whose eyes were still shining,
and we moved towards the stairs.
Before we started walking down

he looked at me
and said softly,
'You should know,
I think your face
is perfection too.'

A Trick of the Light

I no longer filled my kitchen with terrible smells when I brewed my potions. In the freedom of not having to learn in secret as I had to do in the palace where I was watched over by Styx, I could openly create anything I wanted. Thanatos had built me sturdy wooden shelves for all my urns full of herbs. On his trips across the land of the living where he claimed the dead, he brought back herbs and flowers from every corner of the earth. Charon would bring me bone dust, hydra eggshell, blood of the Chimera, the scales of long-dead sirens; all manner of preternatural scraps, which I learned to identify and used in my growing collection of potions, poisons and spells. The knowledge of what all these things were seemed inborn. Soon, the shelves were so heavy that one day Thanatos turned to me in the kitchen after nearly knocking over a potent love potion that could sway a whole village. 'Perhaps it is time to build you an apothecary.' I shook my head. 'You do not have time to help me build an apothecary.' A slow smile formed across his face. 'Then I will *make* the time to build you an apothecary – the dead can wait a little.' I laughed and said, 'You, who never neglects his duties for anyone? I doubt even *I* am worth the God of Peaceful Death neglecting his role.' Thanatos' smile widened and perhaps it was just a trick of the light, but something warm glowed in his eyes. 'You are worth all of it. And more.'

A Visit From Hades

I had not seen him for an era.
Styx had warned me that he was no longer

the gentle boy-God he used to be
but a bitter, paranoid version of himself.

Some said it was the loneliness
of the Underworld that did this to him.

Others said it was because that power
untold, unchecked, had corrupted him.

Either way, his tall, brooding form
appeared in my palace uninvited.

This was a tacit insult. You do not
enter the threshold of another God's domain

without permission. To add further
insult, he had walked into my sanctuary,

the apothecary Thanatos had built me,
while I was working on my poisons.

It was in my examining the brittleness
of old Hydra eggshell that I saw the shadow

in the doorway. I looked up and cold grey eyes
met mine. I asked, 'And what brings the ruler

of this entire realm to my home?'
Hades did not speak. His face looked

chiselled out of old stone by a slightly
careless craftsman, all angles and oddities,

like his too-high eyebrows and too-soft lips.
Then he spoke slowly. 'I am here with a warning.'

The Warning

'When your mother left you here,
you were a child and it was my duty,
as we are all cousins, to see you protected.'

He moved into the room like a snake.
'However, things have taken a turn.'
His grey eyes glinted with a sword's edge.

'Your mother did not tell us the extent of your powers.
If she had, I would have never kept you here.'
I put down the Hydra eggshell on the table.

'How did you know?' I asked him softly.
Despite our schisms, Styx and Pallas
would never have told him of any of this.

Hades looked around the apothecary now,
lifting one of my urns of belladonna,
wrinkling his nose at the smell.

'Hermes told me everything, Hekate.
I know all about your quest. All the Gods are aware,'
he said this quietly, 'of what you are.'

Of course. Hermes. I should have known that
the Olympian in him would not keep
my secrets. The betrayal stung.

I stared at Hades, the curl of distaste
on his mouth jarring and cruel.
'What do you want from me?'

'I am letting you know,'

his voice was so cold,
'that my spies are watching you.'

Charon had told me this about Hades.
He had grown so mistrustful that
he had taken to keeping shadows as spies.

That he deemed me threat enough to have me
watched chilled me to the bone. I stared at him,
unable to fathom this version of him.

'If you had not let me stay, I would have been—'
He cut me off. 'You would be enslaved to Zeus
or Poseidon. Or have turned out like your mother.'

I took in the cold shock of his words.
And then it struck me like ice.
'You are afraid of what I am.'

It was there, in his hesitation
that I knew, but still
I let him speak.

'If you try anything,' his voice was low,
'that challenges my rule. You will wish
that I am as kind to you

as Zeus has been to Prometheus.'

A Calculated Callousness

So it was true. He was not the kind boy-God
he used to be, the one that took me
to my father and called Cerberus off me.

It was said that Hades was greedy
and counted souls like a heartless miser
with gold coins. It was said that he

would have ended the whole world
to increase his bounty of souls.
I had never believed any of this

until now, until he stood there,
his eyes cold with threats and
an unnamed violence.

I did not speak and soon, he left.
But as I watched his retreating form,
a premonition unearthed in my mind:

Something ruthless is on its way
and he is afraid I can stop it.
Why else would he threaten me?

Other Things Take Root

Despite Hades' unsettling visit
I became lost in my work of witchcraft.
I realized I preferred my apothecary

more than necromancy,
my poisons and their antidotes,
basting and anointing, grating

and pasting. Every plant and tree,
even the crystals and rivers, hummed
with untapped power and potential.

I grew more and more lost in my work.
Until one day Thanatos visited
and asked me, 'Do you not think it is time

that you, too, are given worship
and libations to strengthen
your godhood?' I frowned at this,

still mixing sleepy mugwort, airy dandelions
and the drowsy waters of Lethe into a paste
that helped craft dreamless sleep.

I had an apothecary full of potions
I had made to become better at my craft.
Witchcraft was work, practised every day.

'I have no need for those things,'
I scoffed. Thanatos shook his head.
'All Gods require prayer, Hekate.

It is what makes our immortality
tolerable, as it reinforces our power.'
It was odd how my name from his lips

always made my heart beat quicker.
I tried to ignore this by staring
down at the paste as I responded,

'And how do you propose I start
acquiring libations and prayers?'
His eyes were more tired today

than I had ever seen them before.
'Join me at the battlefields of Troy.
The sick and wounded could use

your help.'

Troy

It is a tale as old as Chaos herself. Jealousy. Resentment. Power. Bloodlust and bloodthirst. A quenching so terrible that it leaves behind the scent of nightmares and thunder in its wake. This war was different. A prophecy came to fruition, a visiting prince stole the wife of a Spartan king, said to be the most beautiful woman in the whole world. The reaction was swift, brutal and led to a thousand ships sailing upon Troy and a ten-year war. A decade is a long time to a mortal, but to us, it is over in the blink of an eye. This amount of death, however, demanded all Gods of Death to work hard. Whole families had been ripped apart. The jewel that was once the city of Troy lay in ruins. It was the end of that story that Thanatos had brought me to. I had noticed his hands shake with what he had seen at this war, even if he never spoke of it. A battlefield bathed in twilight smelled of salt and iron. Ground so crimson it was no longer the colour of dirt but rust-red with old blood. Even Troy's great palace, once so grand it was said that Zeus was envious, now lay in smouldering ashes. I tried to ignore the feelings this stirred in me. An old rage, a long-simmering fury threatened to erupt when I saw the crying women and children being loaded onto Greek ships. I wanted to help them but Thanatos placed his hand on my wrist and looked into my eyes. *Not yet.* So instead, I gritted my teeth and went about his work with him. We walked from dying body to dying body and he offered release. All I could do was watch. Watch as he collected soul after soul. I was starting to wonder why he had brought me here when I saw her. The figure of a woman running towards the cliff's edge. A cliff below which were sharp, brutal rocks and an even more merciless sea.

Queen of Ashes and Corpses

I watched her
until her legs gave way
and she collapsed on the cliff's edge.

It was her coronet that gave her away,
her silver hair flowing behind her,
flowing indigo silken dress torn.

This was Hecuba, Queen of Troy.
Leaving Thanatos to his work,
I made my way to her form,

before the Greek soldiers saw her
and did their very worst.
She did not turn to look at me.

'What good is it to be a queen
of ashes and corpses?' she asked,
distraught. I did not respond.

Instead, I waited.
When she turned to me,
I saw the tears streaking her face.

'They killed my husband,
all of my children.
Why did they let me live?'

I knew why they had let her live.
The value of a queen
was higher alive than dead.

In my silence the answer dawned on her.
I saw it in the slow horror
which crept across her features.

It was astounding how cruel
mortals could be towards each other.
All in the name of victory.

I saw the resignation of decision
across her features within a moment,
and she turned back towards the sea.

From the corner of my eye
I could see soldiers approaching.
On the beach below, a crowd gathering.

This was when I knew what to do.
A strange thought came to me and I said,
'I can help you. Let me help you.'

'You cannot help me.'
A broken sob escaped her lips.
'I simply want to see my children again.'

I considered this.
'Your children are in different realms
of the Underworld. You will be able

to see them all if you choose this.'
Her face flitted from despairing to eager.
'It is all I want.' From my bag of simples,

I withdrew a dark blue urn.

The First Boon

I had brewed this on a whim.
My love of Cerberus and what I did
for Argos all those years ago
had driven me to create this potion.

It had sat in my apothecary,
unused and forgotten.
But not knowing what to bring this day,
I had added it to my bag of simples.

'If you drink this,'
I told her, the potent liquid glittering,
'you can roam the Underworld,
see your children whenever you wish.'

She frowned.
'Why would you do this for me?'
I considered her suspicion.
A cold battlefield told her not to trust me.

So I did the only thing I could.
I told her the truth. 'I am Hekate,
Goddess of Witchcraft and Necromancy,
and I believe enough mortals and immortals

have given blood to this war.
And I believe that you deserve
a better future than to be a bed slave
or alone in the fields of Asphodel.'

She reached eagerly for the urn
but I held it tight. 'A warning.

If you drink this you will become
something not of this world.

No longer mortal.
No longer a human form.'
Her hand shook in hesitation
and I continued,

'But you will be under my care
and my protection forever.
You will never know loss again.'
It was those words that did it.

She took the urn and drank.
And then, I watched her turn.
Her silver hair became silver fur.
Her sharp face became a sharp snout.

And before the sun dipped over the horizon
and as the crowd watched below,
she sat before me,
my first sacred animal.

My only silver hound.

A Promise

Nyx cast her spell over the sky,
the dark blue cloak of night fell,
and as the stars appeared
Hecuba nudged my hand.
I turned to Thanatos and said,

'I made her a promise,
that she would meet her children.'
Thanatos looked around the battlefield,
still full with pain. 'My work is not
yet complete. But you should go.'

I would have stayed.
He looked so tired
and it made my heart clench.
But it was my first promise
and first boon to a mortal.

She had lost nineteen children
to this unjust war.
This is what many would call sacrifice.
I called it unnecessary and cruel.
And I could not let her down.

So I left with her. We walked
through the mouth of one cave
out through another
till we were by the greenest
of forests full of bluebird song

and the bright glow of fireflies.
It was said that a spring Goddess
had crafted this forest from barren soil.

As we walked slower now,
marvelling at each fine leaf and flower,
the careful details of an artist,

we heard a terrible sound
rip through the peace.
A loud,
unmistakable
scream.

A Forest Corrupted

It is obscene how often
the cruellest things can happen
in the most beautiful places.

This forest was a sacred jewel
in the crown of a bright,
young spring Goddess.

Even the deer and lambs
lived in peace with
the lions and wolves here.

Hecuba was off like a shot
in the direction of the scream
and I ran after her in pursuit.

And there it was
that I saw the most hideous
of all sights. A young woman,

no, the glow around her body
told me she was a Goddess
screaming as she fought

against the brutal arms
that held her. I ran instantly.
I had to save her!

Hecuba was barking,
alerting me to the chariot
with its fire horses, flaming and majestic.

Before I could reach them,
a sinkhole opened and before
he dragged her into it with him

I saw the face of her assaulter
and recoiled as though slapped.

Hades.

Panic

What do you do when you witness such an awful act? Do you run to the Gods, beg for help? Do you seek out a friend and tell them what has happened? I did neither. I knew what I had witnessed was something so awful its legacy would echo through the land of time forevermore. So I did what I wish I could have done for my mother, pursued by two Gods drunk on their own power. I plotted a rescue. I ran through the forest to the mouth of the cave that would take me to the Underworld. I hurried to my palace, Hecuba at my heels. In my apothecary I piled simples, potions, poisons, anything I could get my hands on. I looked upon Hades' domain, clear as day from my palace tower, and narrowed my eyes, the fury in my chest close to bubbling over. He would not get away with this. I looked at the silver hound and her eyes said everything that was already in my heart. Before I left, I told her to go. Go see her family. I gave her protections, and a spell to show her how to find them, the spirits of her children. And when that was done, I knew what I must do. I would find Hades. He would not get to steal a Goddess and answer to no one. I hefted my bag onto my shoulder and this time, I took the direct route to his palace, Gods in Grey be damned.

I Crossed the Rivers Again

And this time I did not quiver.
There was no doubtful nature to my steps.
There was no hesitation in me.

Even when the foreboding orchard
and its ink-dark fruit menaced me
with its promise of poison.

I was ready. I had a sword crafted
from adamantine, a gift from Charon,
and alongside it, I carried my torch.

I would set his precious orchards alight
if he did not return her to her forest
where she belonged.

I rooted through the orchard
and the tentacles tried to stop me
but I cut and cleared them mercilessly.

Until at the very end
a dark-clad figure stood,
his once-boyish face marred with anger.

My eyes narrowed at him.
'I thought I would find you
hiding here, Hades.'

There Was a Dangerous Glint in His Eye

'I told you to stay away.'
His words dripped with malice.

I gripped my sword tightly.
'I saw what you did.

Send her back now,
and I will leave you in peace.'

His expression turned to amusement.
'You cannot hurt me.'

I lifted my sword in his direction.
'Do not challenge me.'

For a second
there was silence

and then he stepped forward,
rage clouding his features.

'You will do nothing. I took her
by her father Zeus' permission.'

The Sword Fell to My Side

Zeus was the king of the Gods.
His decree was final
and there was very little
I could do to help her.

I closed my eyes, trying to think,
and I remembered his then-young face
when he took me in despite the odds,
when he helped me see my father.

I was sure that somewhere
inside him there lived that boy-God,
the one who let kindness lead him.
If I could just appeal to him instead . . .

'Please, Hades.'
I made my voice soft like honey.
'You are so much better
than your brothers.

Let her go and if she loves you
she will return to you willingly.'
There was a hesitation in his eyes
and I leapt at my chance.

'You are better than this.'

But His Eyes Narrowed

'You forget your place,'
he growled at me.

I should have been afraid,
but his words made me laugh.

'I have never had a place.
What do you think it is

that gives me my courage?'
He turned away from me.

Of course he did,
he had no answer.

As he looked at some
invisible thing,

he said,
'I will not return Kore.

She is destined to be my queen.
And her father gave me permission.'

Kore. Daughter of Demeter,
the Goddess of the Harvest.

So that was who he had stolen.
A child of flowers and innocence.

'Hades.' I softened my tone.
'Think of her mother.

This will destroy her.'
Demeter adored her daughter.

And Kore had never been
without her mother's tenderness.

'Do you not see, she is a spring Goddess
and you have brought her to where nothing grows?'

The more it unravelled in my mind,
the more my heart broke.

'Things do grow here.'
Hades touched a black apple.

'From dead soil and dead bones.
You produce fruit that

no one can eat.'
My hands shook.

'You are taking from her
the very life force she needs.'

But it was no use.
His stubbornness was legendary.

He turned away from me
and walked towards his home.

I glared at his retreating back.
I would see no more daughters

separated from their mothers
on the whims of callous Gods.

If I was to help Kore,
I would have to defy him

and all of his realms.
So be it.

So be it.

The Search

I looked everywhere for her. I searched for what the mortals would call years. The Underworld was no small place, it was a realm of lands within lands. So I used my notes on cartography to seek her out. I visited the midnights of the Realm of Night. I walked through the lavender of the Asphodel Meadows. I even visited the torrid volcanos of Tartarus. None of the banks of the five rivers nor the Elysian Fields had seen her — but I found Hecuba in the Elysian Fields, after she had met with her oldest child, Hector. She did not leave my side, which buoyed my spirits on my fruitless quest. Neither Hades' palace nor orchards revealed anything to me. So it made sense, by the end of this long, exhausting search, that the only place she could be was the Forest of Silence, but I could not enter there without careful planning. When I finally returned to my home, tired and weary, I found Thanatos and Charon waiting for me. I knew by the looks on their faces that they brought with them terrible news.

'What Happened?'

I asked a question
I did not want
to know the answer to.
Neither of them spoke at first.

Thanatos used his staff
to make a crystal orb in the air.
In it I saw nothing.
And then . . . snow.

Villages once brimming
with life full of cold,
dying mortals.

Fields once full of crops
frozen over and lakes
where animals drank
turned to ice.

Everything was dying.
Even the trees had no leaves.
I turned to Thanatos in fear,
'What is this?'

Charon answered,

'Demeter.
Her daughter was taken.
And she will kill the world
unless she gets her back.'

A Mother's Love

is powerful.
It is a force
to be reckoned with.

My mother saved my life.
Demeter would take every life
to get her daughter back.

A mother's love is many things
but most of all it is ancient
and it is destructive

to anything and anyone
that stands between her
and her child.

I chose my words
cautiously.
'I will go see her.'

Charon shook his head.
'You have nothing
to offer her she hasn't heard.'

My smile was cryptic.
'I think I know something
she has not heard before.'

Demeter's Home

was close to Kore's forest.
I once walked her golden fields
marvelling at each ripe,
golden stalk of wheat
shaped so perfectly.

Now it was barren,
the soil so acrid
it reminded me
of the Stygian Marsh,
where nothing could grow.

Her lodgings were in view.
A humble home, still beautiful.
White pillars and white walls.
A courtyard that once,
I imagine, bloomed with flowers.

Even now some crimson petals
lay frozen in the snow.
And there, sitting on the floor,
tears streaming down her face,
was dark-haired, golden-eyed

Demeter herself.

'I Know Where She Is'

Perhaps I should have been
more delicate,

but I could not see a mother
in so much grief.

She reminded me too much
of my own mother.

Demeter looked up
and for a moment,

I thought she would turn me
into ice with her gaze.

Instead, she got up
and moved towards me,

hands on my shoulders
as, wild-eyed, she shook me.

'Where *is* she?'
Oh Hades . . .

What have you done?

'It Was Zeus'

I said it softly, honestly.
Because it was.

Hades may have taken her
but he had done so with the blessing

of Kore's father.
'Zeus gave Hades

permission to take her.
She is in the Underworld,

inside the Forest of Silence.'
The sound that came

from Demeter's throat
was so terrible

I couldn't even name it
a cry of despair.

Her fingers dug
into my shoulders.

'You must take me to her!'
But at this I shook my head.

'You cannot enter
his domain without

his permission,
Goddess of the Living.'

Her face crumpled
into deep agony

and I added quickly,
'Perhaps . . . perhaps

I can return to him
and negotiate some form

of release?'
Demeter's eyes blazed at this.

'I will not negotiate
with the monster who stole

my daughter.
I will turn this world

into nothing. Kill every mortal

that prays to every God.
Leave them diminished

and destroyed if they do not
return my child to me.'

I was quiet as she spoke.
Then I whispered,

'My mother and I
were separated

by the games of Gods too.
Which is why I will try

to get your daughter
back to you.'

Demeter looked into my eyes
as though only just

recognizing who I was.
'Of course. Hekate.'

She touched my cheek
gently now.

'Asteria would be
so proud of you.'

Her Name

It did not wound me to hear it.
Like her memory,
it had become a dull ache.

But Demeter's words
awakened something else
within me.

Only a mother
could truly understand
another mother's pain.

My jaw set as I realized
precisely where
I needed to go.

I took Demeter's hands
in mine and kissed them,
an unspoken promise.

Then I made my way to the cave
that would lead me there.
To Styx's abode.

Reunion

For a long time Pallas and Styx
had not lived together.
Since their children were taken
by Zeus to Olympus,

Styx had seen little point
in living inside an empty home,
so she had returned to her river,
and Pallas had left to roam.

But now, Pallas and Styx had built
a home in which they finally lived
together where the home they
had built for me once stood tall.

A strange pain grasped
my chest when I saw this.
But making something out of ruins
is a powerful kind of practice.

Still, this was the place
where so much began
. . . and ended for me.
Their palace was silver and jade,

the colours of the serpents
Styx cared for.
I had heard her river
ran through its centre,

despite the waters being acrid
and full of spirits.

I wondered what a home
full of poisonous waters was like?

It was time to find out.
Taking a deep breath,
I knocked on the glimmering
silver door.

The Door Opened

and I found myself face to face with Styx.
I know that Gods do not age,
but a pang rose in my chest

at how she looked,
exactly the same
as the day we fought.

Styx stepped back
when she saw me.
'Hekate.'

It wasn't said with surprise
or with anger.
My name sounded like a spell

when she said it that way.
I waited for permission to enter,
and with a nod she gave it to me.

I followed her to a hall split in half
by her own river.
Around me the fine things

that were expected in Gods' houses glowed.
A golden fireplace. Emerald urns.
Thrones crafted from the finest oak.

She snapped her fingers
and a small silver chalice
of sweet wine was in my hand.

'Why Are You Here?'

I hid a smile at her words.
Styx was always pointed.
Clearing my throat I said,
'I went to see Demeter.'

The frown she gave me
would make anyone believe
that I had defied some ancient,
unwritten law.

'Hekate——' she began
but I raised my free hand.
'Listen to me.
You have two young daughters.

Her youngest daughter was taken.
She is in agony.
The whole world
screeches with her pain.

I know where Kore is.
All I am asking for
is your aid.'
I paused and took a sip

of my wine.
Styx was looking at the green flames
in her golden fireplace.
'No. You know I cannot.'

I sighed as I looked at her.
'Why?' I knew the answer

but I wanted her to say
the words to me.

'Hekate, it is against
the rules.' There was
an edge to her voice.
And I finally recognized it.

Fear.

All those rules that she had
for me as a child. Those rules
were not just to keep me safe.
It was the only form of control

a Goddess could have
in this world of Gods.
Her duties. Her rules.
Her world made sense for them.

I was older now. I saw
her for who she was.
And I knew what to say
to change her mind too.

'Imagine,' — my voice was gentle —
'if it was Bia and no one
would tell you where she was.
What would you do?'

I could see her hands
and they clenched into fists.
She could not even stand the thought.
Which was what I expected.

She took a deep breath
and walked over to the black river

that she had nurtured so carefully.
Then she took an emerald urn

and filled it with the water.
Carefully, she brought it to me.
'Use this. It has the power
to dissolve anything in your way

or even steal a God's voice.'
As I reached for it,
her hands did not let it go.
I looked up into her eyes questioningly.

'Hekate. I do not
have two daughters,'
she said softly to me,
'I have three. That includes you.'

Styx's Words

filled an abyss inside me
that I had been guarding,
pretending that it did not exist.

Walking away from her
and Pallas in rage
had made me feel like I had

no way to return to them.
But I thought I knew better now.
I assumed what they did

was only to protect me
but also in penance
towards my parents.

What I did not realize
was that Styx actually loved me.
Here was confirmation

that I may have lost
my own mother,
but I was not motherless

and nor was I alone.

Fear

I had barely taken a few steps
out of Styx's palace
when I heard it,
the sound of small wings,

a breathlessness
a flash of gold,
and I looked up to see
Hermes.

He landed before me
but before I could greet him
I saw his face,
a fear in his voice.

What would make
Hermes the Olympian,
Hermes the arrogant,
afraid . . .

He stumbled forward
and I caught him
before he fell,
his elegance a distant memory.

He clutched my arms
as, terrified, he looked
into my eyes.
'War . . . war has come to Olympus.'

That Word

It was a cruel haunting.
The story of my childhood destroyed,
the trauma of my parents lost,
all connected to that one word,
a single, three-letter word:

War.

Of course there had been wars
between mortals,
the Gods ensured it.
But this?
This was different.

I knew without Hermes telling me
that this was a darker thing.
Another war between immortals
that could devastate the
order of everything we had become used to.

A part of me was terrified.
And yet there was a smaller part,
a vengeful, simmering fury
that looked at his fear,
the same panic he and his had inflicted

on my family and thought,

Good.

'You Have to Help Us'

I frowned at his words.
What could he possibly mean?

'The giants. They have
found their way onto Olympus

and even Zeus cannot
defeat them. We are weakened.

Demeter's destruction
has taken too many mortal lives.

There are not enough
humans left to pray to us

and without their prayers
our powers have been failing.

We need your help.'
I stood stock-still.

My body was cold
and I let him go.

'Why would the giants
go to war *now*?'

He shook his head impatiently.
'Power. They too are Kronos'

children, do you not remember?'

I gave him a wry smile. 'I do not know
if you have noticed, but we have

a few too many cousins
to keep track of.'

Hermes glared at me.
'This is not the time for humour.'

The trickster God saying this
brought home the urgency.

'Tell me more, Hermes.
If I am to help, I need knowledge.'

I could see the conflict
play across his face.

To trust me with more information
could prove fatal for the Olympians,

but to not give me information
was to spurn my aid.

Finally, I saw him relent.
'For years the giants

have kept to themselves.
But they have always

been power-hungry.
What happened during

the last war has kept them
in their place. Still, to keep them

content enough to prevent
another war, my father Zeus

made a series of oaths with them.
They are mortal, so he gave them

longevity. But they believe that Olympus
holds secrets to immortality.

To rule would mean power forever,
and they are tired of dying.'

I sighed and said softly, 'The price
of that crown is the constant threat of war.

I hope all that you are protecting
is worth it in the end.'

He scowled at me.
'Are you going to help?'

'Ask Hades.
He is powerful enough—'

As I began to say this
he was already shaking his head.

'I have already seen Hades.
He says that the affairs

of Olympus are for Olympus
to resolve.'

I nodded quietly,
'He is correct.'

That fearful look was back
in Hermes' eyes.

'Hekate, you don't understand.
If Olympus falls,

where do you think
the giants will turn to next?'

My Home, the Underworld, Was in Danger

Thoughts were moving so fast
within my mind that I could barely
hold onto a single thread.

Was I really going to help them?
After everything they had
put my parents through?

Each thought gave way to the next
until finally I felt and saw it.
It was a dangerous idea.

It had a thousand ways
of going very, very wrong.
But it *was* a way.

So I turned to Hermes
and said carefully,
'We must go to the Realm of Night.'

Hermes was about to protest.
He feared Nyx as all Gods do.
'We are not going to see Nyx, *surely.*'

I shook my head,
'Indeed we are not.
We are going to see Thanatos.'

Thanatos' Home

This time I knew to avoid Kronos' cave. I knew which path to take. I knew how to light a torch to keep the creatures that lived in those caves at bay. Everything here had sharp fangs and a taste for ichor and iron equally. I led Hermes through the caves to the open realm of darkness. The fog was thick around the entrance to Night, another of Nyx's tests. I used some of Styx's waters on my torch, causing the flames to turn an emerald green, which quickly chased the fog away. Hermes was not speaking, something I had thought impossible. He followed at my heels with an obedience I had only seen from my hound since I had found her in the Elysian Fields. It made me quicken my pace. This was a dangerous moment in the history of the Gods; one misstep could lead to another ten-thousand-year war. Thanatos' palace was made from the finest pieces of both nightmares and dreams. Impossible stones that glowed both onyx and iridescent. A garden of a kind with black grass, crimson crystal roses emerging from the skeletal remains of a perfectly formed large dragon. High towers surrounded by storm clouds that should not exist down here. I had once asked what the doors were made of, assuming they were ivory. Thanatos had smiled and told me that they were made from his favourite kind of jewel. Human bone.

'What Are You Doing Here?'

His voice carried to us
and we turned. He had been standing
at the head of his dragon,
preparing to plant more roses.

A rose for every mortal that died.
This place was more red than black now.
It was tender in the way Thanatos
did not like to admit that he was.

'I need your permission,'
I said as we approached him.
Hermes, to his credit, was still quiet.
Thanatos smiled only at me.

'What kind of permission is that?'
Thanatos asked me easily,
but he was looking at Hermes
with a deep suspicion.

'There is another immortal war
about to erupt and *I need your permission*,'
I repeated, this time with emphasis.
His eyes widened as Hermes nodded,

testifying to my words.
'How can I help, Hekate?'
Thanatos' voice was firm now.
I smiled at him and told him my plan.

We Began Our Journey

The lands of the living were starting to look like the lands of the dead. Bodies littered across fields and villages, covered in ice and snow. Which was precisely what I needed. It was in my own cold divinity that I had thought of this idea, an idea that had made Hermes smirk even through his fear and Thanatos gaze at me long enough that I recognized my own callousness. But I took their reactions the way I had learned to take all reactions from Gods. With a grain of salt. We walked through the lands, Hecuba by my side. For comfort, I would sometimes stroke her white fur absently as we saw body after body and she whined. I pulled out my bag of simples, and worked quickly. Moly and mugwort, lavender and bone dust, the amber hearts of newborn stars. It came so quickly to me now, my craft considered anathema to the Gods. Hermes and Thanatos watched me silently as I worked. Now at the very last village, obliterated by the cold, I gently placed the last heart I had into the chest of a blue corpse. He rose as the others did from the endless sleep of death back into a half-life. Stepping back, I surveyed them all. Once, they were human. Now, touched by divinity, they were an abomination to every other God. But to me, they were my own beautiful, merciless creations. I named them for what they were.

I called them Legion.

Legion

It was a plan full of risk.
More likely failure.

But it was all we had left.
The giants were powerful

and the Gods were weakening.
So I looked upon my thousands,

once corpses left to decay.
They stood impossibly before me

blinking into the cold and grey
that no longer affected them,

watching silently, none speaking.
Hermes whispered to me,

'You are their maker, Hekate.
Give them your command.'

It struck me in that moment.
This was my army.

I was now
their general.

And we were going
to war.

I Breathed in the Cold Deeply

for I had to harden my heart
to what I had become.
Once my world was wrecked by war.
Now I was a leader in one.

Somewhere, I was sure,
the Fates were laughing.
But there was no time to reflect
on the complexities of immortality.

Instead, I turned to this army
I had created and said loudly,
'I have brought you back for a purpose.
The realms of the Gods are under attack.

This means the very nature of this world,
any loved ones you may have left,
even the afterlife you walk into,
is under threat of extinction.'

A murmur rose now:
they could speak.
At least they remembered
some of their humanity.

'I am asking for your help.
I am asking you to march
with me upon Olympus,
where giants have laid siege.'

The murmurs grew louder.
I could feel Thanatos' eyes

upon me as I spoke.
I heard Hermes' slow chuckle.

An impossible plan
for an impossible army.
'In return, if we win,' I continued,
'I can offer you a second life,

one of more comfort than you knew.'
At this the army grew so loud
that Hecuba started barking.
The heat of excitement battled

both the cold and the decay.
I heard Hermes clear his throat.
This was not something I could offer;
only Zeus could bestow this wish.

But I fully intended to make Zeus
accept this as my boon.
Besides, would it not benefit
the Gods to have more mortals

left that would pray to them?
I turned back to my army,
blue-skinned, held together
by the hearts of stars.

'What say you?' I call,
and the roar of agreement
that followed steeled my spine.
'Then onward we march!'

Thanatos' Words

'Hekate.' His voice was soft
as we led the legions,
soft enough that Hermes,
walking close by, could not hear.

I looked at him and his kind eyes
held a thousand years of concern.
'Tell me,' he asked softly,
'that you are sure you want to do this.'

I knew what he was asking.
Thanatos knew about my parents.
He knew how much I had
hated the Titanomachy.

And he was right. What was I doing?
Was I truly going to lead an army
to protect the same Olympians
who had caused me such pain?

Who had driven my mother
out to sea after abandoning me?
And locked my father into
a prison made of torture?

Was I ready to face
who I would be after I had led
a war? What if another child
was left abandoned after this?

And that would be my fault.

But if everything fell into place
according to my plan,
this would be less of a war,
more of a surprise attack.

And one thing I knew,
about the element of surprise:
if executed properly,
this would be over quickly.

I turned to Thanatos
and smiled reassuringly,
despite my own worries.
'Yes. Yes I am sure.'

To Olympus

I had been purposeful in my actions.
When I chose that last village,
it was the closest to the godly mountains.

And now, not even a few miles
through the sleet and ice and snow,
I saw the beauty of a falling Olympus.

I had never been there,
but a golden mountain powered
by ichor was impossible not to see.

It stood out like an exquisite atrocity
among the peaceful grey of the others.
Storm clouds and lightning

surrounded the top of the mountain,
obscuring the Gods' abode from view.
But we heard the thunder, the roars,

even from this distance,
the silhouettes of the behemoths
that were called giants visible,

legs and arms so large
that they made the mountain
look like a large oak they were climbing.

My jaw set as we kept walking.
There was no time to waste.
We must start climbing. But first . . .

A Task

'Why have we stopped?'
asked Hermes impatiently,
his voice curdled with annoyance.

I frowned at him,
standing beside a calm Thanatos.
Behind them my beautiful creatures

remained silent and still,
waiting for my next command.
'It is not wise,' I said quietly,

'to march into a war
without intelligence or a plan.
Perhaps your sister Athena

could have told you that.'
Hermes' eyes narrowed
with churlish impatience as he said,

'My sister is battling monsters at present,
so we have not had the pleasure
of discussing the art of war.'

Thanatos' voice broke between us,
his tone even, peace-making.
'What Hekate is saying, Hermes,

is that you should use those wings
and give us some wisdom
of the view at the very top.'

To Hermes' credit
he did not fight back.
In fact, I almost wondered

if he had been expecting this,
for he instantly looked up at Olympus
and said, 'Do not move from here.

I will return shortly.'
And like the quicksilver tongue
he was known for,

he was gone.

As We Waited, I Felt It

The chill of what
I was about to do.

There would be blood, and pain.
Once again my family would fight

each other, for even the giants
were our cousins.

And this time, I would lead an army
the way my father did.

What if we lose?
'We will not lose.'

Thanatos' gentle voice
broke through my panic.

I felt his hand softly take mine
and I turned to him.

'You have enough fire inside you
to win a thousand wars,

you will win this
and the next one too.'

'I do not want any more wars,'
I told him. He smiled sadly and

pulled me closer and I sank into his arms.

The View From the Top

Hermes was gone less than half a day. In this time, we settled the army down at the base of the mountain where the giants could not see us. A blind spot, Hermes had called it before he had left. The undead felt no cold and needed no food in their liminal state, so instead, stayed quiet, the hearts of beating stars inside them. I could not look at them for long before my guilt began to sing too loudly. So instead, we waited in silence together. Finally Hermes returned, his face grim and carefully blank as he narrated the state of the war in the skies. The giants had done great damage to the defences of Olympus. The pillars that once stood for millennia were in pieces. Hephaestus had been captured and there was no more adamantine for the Gods to use as weapons. Ares' red storm had failed to do any damage. Zeus' thunderbolts and lightning were no match against the size of the giants, and had only wounded a few of them. Hera had been captured and was being held hostage by two of the biggest giants. Poseidon had been cornered into a place he could not summon water to his aid. Apollo and Artemis had been flung off the mountain and were fighting their way back up. Athena was the only reason the Gods had not surrendered yet — her warcraft had created an invisible army to stop the giants from destroying the centre of Olympus and the altars of the Gods. Time was running out. Another half day and all would be lost.

Thanatos Speaks

Terror should have been gripping me,
but I had no moment to spare for it.
The Olympians were more powerful than me.
I took a step back from Hermes
and nearly fell back into Thanatos' arms.

'How do I do this?' I asked him,
'I have never led an army,
I do not know the art of war.'
His kind, tired eyes looked upon me.
'Do you know why I agreed to help you?

Or even,' he said, glancing at Hermes,
'why Hermes came to you for aid?'
I shook my head quietly.
'Hekate. You are the only divinity
who has faced violent giant blood

and lived to tell that story.'

I Took a Step Back From Him

'What?' I asked in confusion.
Hermes spoke now.
'You fought Kronos.
You survived him.'

I had forgotten about Kronos.
I had forgotten about
how he was the maker of giants.
How he had made them

of Ouranous' blood
in his very own image.
They were meant to be
Kronos' personal army.

Until, at the very end
of the Titanomachy,
Zeus promised them freedom
in exchange for giving up their master.

Kronos had nearly trapped me,
until one version of me had taken a torch
and thrust it into his face,
the heat from the fire rescuing me.

I had not forgotten what it took
to make him very, very afraid.
'Torches,' I said softly to them.
'We need torches, hundreds of them.'

Looking back at my army,
I amended my words.
'We need *thousands*.'

Climbing a Golden Mountain

I had never been more grateful
to have the powers of a Goddess
than in the moment where we
turned damp pieces of wood
into torches with a touch.

If we were mortal, this would take
a hundred days or more,
but for Gods it was effortless.
Within moments of my suggestion
thousands of torches had been formed

and handed to the army behind us.
And this was when we began our climb.
From above, heavy marble pillars
fell past us, and the smell of sweet
ambrosian God-blood grew thick.

I felt a sickness as I climbed
and the smell of ichor and iron
grew stronger, reminding me of
Tartarus, where my father was trapped.
I was climbing a mountain full of his blood.

I pushed this thought away brutally
as the climb grew steeper
and we had to use our hands
as much as our legs to rise.
Finally, my hand reached up
and I touched cold, smooth floor.

Olympus Was Burning

When Hermes described this
he had failed to mention
the sheer scale of the carnage.

Red and gold blood caked the floor.
The Gods were immortal
but the giants were numerous

and only a few massive bodies lay
among the crumbling
marble of immaculately made

and once-seemingly invincible pillars.
Ares's red storm was waning
and Zeus was high in the sky.

Athena looked to be tiring,
fighting them back from the altars
where the prayer-smoke was starting to die.

Without a moment lost,
I crawled forward to make way
for the army behind me,

and then carefully whispered
the words that would set
every single one of our torches alight.

'γενηθήτω φῶς!
Let there be light!'

The Advance

The giants were distracted
and consumed with near-victory.

'We will not get a better chance,'
I whispered to Thanatos and Hermes.

'They are afraid of fire,'
I said softly, and the whisper

passed down the ranks.
'Use your torches in their faces,

burn their toes, their eyes.
I have blessed you with unending flame.'

And with these words,
I looked upon the giant closest to me,

the one who was destroying
the altar with Hera's sigil,

and crept up behind him
before he could see me.

The Element of Surprise

It was all we had.
The hope that the giants were

unprepared

for what we brought into the fray
and that our damage

was brutal

and swift enough
to force their retreat.

I put myself ahead of my army,
for it was my knowledge

that had brought us here,

and it was only fair
that I took the first risk.

I leapt to the huge being,

as tall as the pillar
he had lifted into his arms,

and I used my torch on his shin.

Battle

A roar ripped from the giant's throat
as he looked down at me,
and his comical cry drove my fear away.
I smiled up at him insolently
as I twirled my two fiery torches.

He dropped the pillar with a hard thud,
Hera's sigil crumbling.
Ungainly now, he reached down.
But I was prepared.
I climbed on top of

the closest pile of debris
and as he reached for me
I burned his fingers,
and while he snatched them back,
I set his loincloth aflame.

Shrieking, the great being
tumbled backwards
all the way off the edge.
I heard his roar as he plummeted
to the ground, a distant cry of dismay.

I felt a cry of triumph
bursting within my blood.
All around me the giants were falling.
My army of dead had turned this battle,
there was a chance we may win!

When I turned back I saw
Thanatos upon the back of
one of the giants,

about to shove the torch
into his face.

But before he could do it
the creature grabbed Thanatos
off his back, as though he were
one of Pallas' carved toys,
and threw him across Olympus
till his back met a pillar and he slid

to the ground.

'THANATOS!'

I screamed, a white-hot fear bursting through my chest. I raced across the mountaintop. When I reached him, Thanatos looked up at me, eyes wide in confusion and pain. I tried to help him stand up but he shook his head slightly and winced. I moved my hand to the back of his head, and my fingers came away with ichor. This is when the fear inside me changed to red-raw rage. I knew Thanatos would heal eventually, as all Gods do. But that creature had the gall to make him bleed. The idea of more Titan blood spilling on this unholy mountain made me pick up my torches and turn. My eyes met with the giant who had done this and with a cry of fury, I raced towards him. In my peripheral vision I saw Hermes battling two giants alongside my undead army. He turned just in time to watch me as once again I split into my timeless three. All three of us with our six torches leapt upon the giant, knocking him to the ground and shoving our flames into his eyes. The creature screamed in agony and struggled, trying to throw us off, but my rage had given us the strength of a thousand lions each. When the giant was finally dead, I looked at the two other versions of me that had come from my bones and sinew, before turning back to Thanatos, who was walking towards us. My heart lightened with relief as I realized he was recovered. He picked up a torch. Wordlessly, we all headed into the heart of Olympus where the Olympians had been cornered into their very last stand.

The Last Stand of the Olympian Gods

Years from now, when they tell this story,
pieces of it will be changed to erase
the truth: that it was an army of undead mortals
that saved the Gods in their last stand.

Even though my Legion soldiers fought till their
star-hearts began to flicker,
fought for unworthy Gods
with their blue hands and torches.

The tale will also forget that in the ruins
of Zeus' once-fine palace, he battled
with an ever-dwindling quiver of thunderbolts.
That Ares was beaten so much,

he could barely move. That Athena's
famous shield and spear lay broken
on the floor as she was left with her fists
alone against three angry giants.

Indeed, the story told will say the Gods
always had the upper hand.
That the giants were simply fortunate
they were able to get this far.

But what they would never erase
is the story of a Goddess who knew
how to raise the dead into an army,
marching upon thousands of giants

with the God of Death and the Trickster
by her side, with the torches and flames
that would finally bring the giants
to their knees and cause them to flee.

Aftermath

It was strange to stand again upon rubble that was once a palace. I had known the wreckage of palaces well. I was once a child who ran through a crumbling home, learning about a world beyond its walls that was covered in golden blood. I now knew what made the floors of this place gold and it invoked a bitterness in me. The sweet-burned smell of ichor was so pungent, I could not wait to return to the Underworld. But first I helped Ares recover his mother, Hera, from the edge of Olympus, distracting her captors with my torches as she freed herself from their chains. Thanatos went to find Hephaestus, locating him in the bowels of his mountain forge, locked away in a box they had forced him to craft. Hermes aided Apollo and Artemis in their return to the mountain, but not before they had sliced through the ankles of enough giants still climbing the mountainside and sent them tumbling. And Zeus helped Athena recover what was left of the altars for rebuilding. My army was back with me, thousands covering the mountaintop, nearly spilling over its edges. In the end, we stood upon the smoking ruins as all the Olympians assembled. They were beautiful, as all the legends said. Arrogant and powerful and yet . . . yet they had needed help from me. It was Zeus who spoke first. 'Hekate, daughter of Asteria and Perses. Your efforts have served us well. For this, we will give you anything you ask.'

The First of My Boons

I had been expecting these words,
and yet I did not speak instantly.
Instead, I was careful with my answer.

'The mortals that aided us.
The ones I brought back to help you.
Give them the ability to live again,

in comfort. For their services.'
I watched the faces of the Olympians
as they slowly processed this.

They could not fathom
a Goddess who cared about mortals.
To them, mortals were so insignificant

that they had made it a game
of playing with their lives.
But like my uncle Prometheus

before me, I saw a beauty
in humans. They were doomed
and yet still lived such full lives.

Zeus traded an unreadable look
with Poseidon. Then after what felt
like a thousand years, he looked at me

and nodded. 'So granted.'
I bowed my head in thanks,
but did not move. Zeus raised his brow.

'I am not finished,' I said.
'Hermes and Thanatos, please,
if you could lead my army away.'

Hermes grinned at me
and Thanatos nodded,
and I watched as they led

my star-hearted mortals away.

The Second of My Boons

Zeus waited until the last mortal's hand
had left the edge of the mountain.
Then he looked at me and said,
'What do you want for yourself?'

I knew what I wanted,
but I did not know if it was possible.
I stared down at the obscene gold floors
and then met his stare steadily.

'I want you to free my father
and his brothers from their punishment.'
A loud, dark silence fell
across this devastated realm.

'That,' Zeus responded, his voice
laced with danger, 'is not possible.'
But another voice interrupted him.
'It *is* possible if you so desire, God-King.'

Hera stepped between me and her husband.
'We have lived with the guilt of this
under our feet for long enough.
Besides that, this mountain shining gold

is what made it such an easy mark.'
Zeus looked like he might argue this.
But instead, he sighed and nodded.
'I will release them from the blood-let.

But *not*,' he added firmly, 'from Tartarus.'

The Third of My Boons

It was more than I could have hoped for.
I was expecting a direct refusal.
At least this meant my father
would be finally free from torture.

And Tartarus was unpleasant,
but at least he would not have to bleed
for the pleasure of his enemies anymore.
I took a deep breath and said,

'I thank you. I have one more request.'
Zeus' face distorted into a scowl.
'You push too far, Titanide.'
A warning. A threat.

I held my ground.
'My final request is for Gods and mortals alike,'
I said softly. 'Mortals are dying
and your powers are dying with them.

It is Demeter's winter that is killing them.
Let her have her daughter back, oh Zeus.
Let them be reunited and order be restored.'
I watched his face as I said this.

At first there was annoyance at me,
then a wave of grudging understanding.
And finally, at long last,
Zeus spoke again.

'I will allow it.
But only

if she has not eaten anything
in the land of the dead.'

A caveat. Constraints.
I wondered if this was his trick.
While Gods did not need food,
we did eat for pleasure often.

And everything I had heard
of Kore spoke of joy and kindness
and yes, even of pleasure.
She was a Goddess of spring,

used to fruits every day
for her meals. But I could not argue.
I had used all of my cards here.
I nodded and just as I was about to leave,

Zeus said to me,
'Hekate, tarry.'
I stopped but did not turn back.
'I never want to see you

anywhere near this mountain again.'
I closed my eyes at these words.
Gods are not good with fear,
and I had proven myself worthy of their fear.

'One more thing.' Zeus' voice rang out.
'You must never marry.
Especially not a child of the night.
Especially not Thanatos.'

My eyes widened and I spun back
at his words. His stony gaze met mine
and I realized he knew something
I had refused to admit to myself

until this moment. That Thanatos
meant so much more to me
than just friend. I did not speak.
I turned away, not giving Zeus

the satisfaction of agreement.

A Cruel Demand

As I made my way down Olympus
I turned over Zeus' words inside my head
as though they were a stone in my hand.

'You must never marry.
Especially not Thanatos.'
Especially not Thanatos.

Why had I not seen it clearly,
what was brewing between us?
And how had Zeus known?

And why? *Why could I never marry?*
And then I realized why.
My gifts. Witchcraft. Necromancy.

These were not gifts Olympians
were blessed with, and powers
they did not know, they feared.

Zeus was not just afraid of me.
He was afraid of what my children
might do to his rule.

Especially if I had a child
with Thanatos, a son of Nyx,
the only Goddess Zeus feared.

To prevent even the idea of an uprising,
Zeus had taken Styx's and Pallas' children.
But our offspring would pose a greater threat to him.

For he had no control over us.
Unlike Styx and Pallas, Thanatos and I
had not declared loyalty to Zeus.

A Return

Styx was waiting for me at the mouth
of her river's cave. Her long green tresses
were loose again as they always were
when she was tending to the souls
in her waters. She saw me approach
and rose, her dress' hem wet
and her eyes full of questions.

'I must find Kore.'
I told her quickly of Zeus,
the Boons and his conditions
on Kore's return to her mother.
She listened carefully and nodded.
'I will come with you.'
I was about to protest

but a single glare from her silenced me.
Charon appeared upon his ferry.
I could already see Styx's acidic waters
damaging his small boat.
But he smiled, his eyes reassuring,
and gestured open-handed
for us to jump in.

We did as he asked
and he moved us with the speed
he would move Gods,
not the mortal souls he was used to.
Quickly the rapids were gone
and we were standing at
the banks of the Forest of Silence.

Back in the Forest of Silence

It was so quiet here
that the sound of her sobs
echoed around us mournfully.

'She is at the centre,'
Styx grimaced.
I knew this, and yet

I had hoped
she would be closer.
But Hades was clever.

He knew that someone
would come looking for her,
and no one survived this forest.

Well. *Almost* no one.

Styx and I walked to the edge of the trees
and we heard the tendrils,
the serpents, before we saw them.

But Styx was ready,
and from her hands
came the poisonous waters

even the Gods feared.
I stood back as she bore a hole
through the forest,

killing murderous roots
of poisonous tree-mockeries
and chasing snakes away.

If I had thought walking here
with Thanatos was safe,
Styx made me feel invincible.

Kore

We ran through the woods,
the sound of our racing feet
mingling with the sound of her sobs
louder and louder until it felt
like the heartbeat of Chaos herself.

Finally we reached the centre
of the forest, a stone cottage,
grey and cold, unlike anything
Kore could ever be used to.
I swallowed my anger

and together, Styx and I
walked into the cottage.
We found the girl sitting
at a stone table, tears falling
down her face.

She looked up at us
in surprise
and her tears stopped.
'Kore,' Styx said,
'we have come to help.'

But I said nothing.
My eyes were locked
upon the plate before her.
A single pomegranate burst open.
A seed in her hand, the juice

red as blood on her lips.

'We Are Too Late'

The words felt heavy in my mouth.
As though I was dropping a weight
onto the world.

The plate sat there,
taunting us.
Kore stood up,

her lovely red hair falling
to her waist as she asked,
wide-eyed and innocent,

'What are you saying?'
I swallowed the hot tears
at the back of my throat.

I was going to break her heart.
And then I would break
Demeter's heart too.

'I . . . I am sorry.
I was supposed to take you home.
But the condition was

that you had not eaten
a single thing in
the land of the dead.'

There was an awful silence.
And then the girl let out
a terrible cry of despair.

Her hand picked up the plate
and she smashed it
to pieces across the floor.

She sank to her knees
and we stood there
helpless, unable to do anything

but watch
as rivers of misery
flowed down the girl's face.

A Voice in the Darkness

It startled us all . . .
The sound of a deep abyss
coming from the door.

'All is not lost.'
I turned to see Hades
standing at the door.

His head was bowed.
If I did not know Gods better,
I would almost say I saw guilt.

He walked into the room,
his gait was slow,
Kore had stopped crying.

Instead, she was staring at him
with exhaustion and suspicion.
He kneeled beside her

and reached to touch her face.
She edged back from his touch.
He sighed and withdrew his hand.

'All is not lost,'
he said again,
his eyes full of longing.

'How much of the pomegranate
did you eat, Kore?'
he asked her tenderly.

I could see he loved the girl.
But in his desire he had not cared
what she wanted,

not understood the damage
he was bringing upon them both.
A marriage should not begin this way.

Kore answered quietly,
'Six seeds.' Even now, full of fear
and anger, her voice was gentle.

'Six seeds.' Hades looked crestfallen
and then said softly,
'This gives you two seasons

with your mother.
Would that please you?'
His face was so hopeful.

Kore's eyes narrowed.
'And the rest of the seasons?'
she asked him pointedly.

He sighed and said,
'You will rule here
with me. As my queen.'

Kore's face crumpled for a second.
But then I watched a Goddess
being born.

She looked him in his eyes
and told him,
'I will agree to this.

However, I will only
accept this if you bestow
half your entire realm to me.

If I am to be your queen,
I will be your equal.
You will take no other lovers.'

Hades looked surprised
at these words,
and for a moment,

I thought he would refuse.
But to my surprise,
he smiled and nodded.

Kore wiped her eyes
on the back of her hand
and drew herself up

to her full height.
Hades nodded at Styx,
then spoke to me.

'Hekate, I ask you
to be Kore's escort.
Please take her home.'

Styx Took Kore Out of the Cottage

but I lingered for a moment,
looking at Hades' form,
half-covered in shadow.

For a moment neither of us
uttered a single sound,
but finally I had to ask.

'What convinced you to let her go?'
My words hung heavy in the air
as I saw his pale face,

tired in the dim light.
'I wanted,' he said slowly,
'to be better than my brothers.'

I waited. So he continued.
'At the end of that war,
I no longer recognized them.

Their wants and desires
overtook their initial will
of overthrowing Kronos to do good.

If I treat Kore like a possession,
force her into my arms and my bed,
how am I any different?'

He looked out the door
to where Styx and she waited.
'Keep her safe, Hekate.'

This was all I needed to hear.

I smiled at Hades.
Perhaps that tender part of him

was not dead after all.

A Mother's Love

I cannot remember how we reached Demeter's cottage. Only that the miles fell away quickly beneath our feet. She was sitting where I left her, heartbroken and staring at frozen hands she refused to warm up. Before we had even reached the footpath, Kore had broken into a run. 'Mama!' she shouted, and I watched as Demeter looked up, as though she was in a dream. Her face held everything. Shock, then relief and then the boundless beauty of joy. She got up from her stoop and as she did, it was as though the whole of winter fled. Gone was the icy wind with each footstep to her daughter. Gone was the snow with each of her smiles. Gone was the chill and the cold replaced with the warmth of spring, a thousand plants bursting out of the ice-covered ground as mother and daughter met and held each other. It was as though the world reset before my eyes. Bluebirds were singing, a gentle doe sprinted across the fields and behind me the forest was full of insects and lush green trees and the scent of a thousand flowers again. I stayed for a few moments. Stayed to watch Demeter and Kore's happiness at being reunited. At last, a mother and daughter who had not been forced apart forever. I took in a deep breath of this joy, a joy that would never be mine. And as I was about to turn and leave, Demeter's voice came to me like flowers upon the breeze. 'Thank you, Hekate.'

The Forbidden Journey

Perhaps it was because I
had become too mistrustful.

Perhaps it was because Zeus
had been so reluctant with this.

But I had to see for myself.
I had to make sure that my father

and all his brothers were free
from their brutal bloodletting

before I allowed myself
to go home and rest.

So I made the forbidden journey
all the way to Tartarus.

I could not find a way
inside the chambers,

but if Zeus kept his promise,
I would at least be able to see

my father from above
the mountain of fire.

I had learned a spell for flight
over my years of witchcraft.

So I rose to the top of the mountain
and gazed down to search within

the depth of Tartarus.
At first I did not see him

among his dazed brothers
and cousins. But then

I saw him. Huge and glowing,
still covered in ichor,

he was walking out
of his prison, safe.

I willed him to look up,
to see me one last time.

But he did not. I stayed as long as I could
and just as I was about to leave,

I heard a voice behind me say,
'Did you doubt Zeus

would keep his word?'
I turned to see Hermes

flying behind me,
a large set of ichor-covered keys

in his hand. He grinned at me.
'I freed them myself, Hekate.'

I smiled slightly back at him,
my exhaustion starting

to make my spell wane.
'Thank you, Hermes.'

He nodded, and as I was
about to fly away, he said,

'I hope one day you trust me
and we can be friends again.'

My smile widened as
I turned to him,

'You were a friend today, Hermes.
I will not forget that anytime soon.'

And with that I started to descend
so I could begin my long journey

to my palace
on the other side of the Underworld.

Home

Thanatos was waiting for me
when I returned.

He was sitting with Hecuba
on the stairs of my home,

his hand gently stroking her head
as it lay in his lap.

I looked at him and a sharp pain
erupted in my heart.

He smiled at me when he saw me,
but when I did not smile back,

he frowned and asked,
'What ails you?'

If I had it in me to cry,
I would have wept in this moment.

But instead, I took a breath and
I told him of what Zeus had asked.

He listened to my words carefully,
then walked towards me,

and took my face in his hands.
I closed my eyes at the warmth of his touch.

'We are Titans. Fuck Zeus. Fuck his customs.
Fuck his marriages and Olympus.

We are not governed by them.
We will do exactly what we please.'

I looked into his eyes
and just like that,

a resolve formed in my mind.
He was right. We answered to no one,

not even God-Kings.
I had already defied Hades.

I would defy Zeus too.
I would defy the world

if it meant I could be with Thanatos.
It occurred to me with a jolt then:

I loved him. I *truly* loved him.
I lifted my head from his hands

and it was then that I realized
that our lips were so close.

This was the closest we had ever been.
I moved first. Or maybe he did.

My lips touched his gently,
and like a long-held promise,

his mouth yielded to mine
and suddenly it was as though

a thousand stars were born,
every river, every ocean in the world

stopped flowing for a second for us,

even the moon in all her glory
stopped her glow to stare at us.

And when we finally parted for air,
The world, the universe, everything

made sense. And then he smiled at me
and my heart melted. I smiled back.

It was Hecuba's bark
that broke our gaze.

Thanatos laughed.
Then he took my hand.

'Come inside. Styx and Pallas
and Charon are all waiting.'

There is, of course,
more to the story.

But that is a tale
For another time.

As of now, we must part.
You see, my family awaits me.

Epilogue

There are a thousand stories
about a wandering island.

Some will tell you how once
a Goddess named Leto gave birth

to twin Gods here.
How the sister who came first

helped her mother birth
her infant brother.

Some will tell you
how the herbs that grow here

are so divine that no mortal
is allowed on this island.

But only a few will tell you
of the Goddess.

The Goddess that was pursued
to the point that she

had to give up her only child.
The Goddess that when given

the choice between
servitude and cruelty

forged her own path
by becoming something else.

That is another story only a few know.
Some may tell you about

the Goddess who visits the island.
A tall, willowy woman

who holds three faces
and three bodies inside her bones.

They say that every full moon
she walks across this island's beaches

and the wind in the trees carries
the island's secret voice to her.

A voice that holds falling stars
and ancient prophecies inside itself.

My daughter, you have honoured me
in ways I could never even have dreamed.

Acknowledgements

This book, all of it, came to me as a vivid dream that would not leave me alone until every word was written down. It is a story I have lived with for years with characters I have talked about and built in real time. The people I love most and the people who believed in this story the most therefore deserve my deepest gratitude first and foremost.

To Nikesh, Nerm and Anoushka, who continue to be the kindest friends one could hope for, thank you for standing by me through everything. You are family forever to me.

To Zubin, who asked me why this book didn't exist yet and encouraged me to write it, and to Mo, for asking me all the best questions about it, thank you for being the best.

To Steve, who has stood by me through every word, every worry big or small and who has always known precisely what I need precisely when I need it. Thank you for holding my hand and not letting go.

To my agent Niki Chang, who has always been my champion and the best agent I could have asked for, thank you endlessly for believing in my work. To David Evans and Sophia Rahim, who were the first to read *Hekate* and give the book so much love — validating my long journey writing it — thank you from the bottom of my heart.

To Charlotte Trumble, for being so passionate about Hekate's story and for such an incredible editorial journey, thank you! To Margaret Raymo, for your deeply encouraging edits and holding Hekate's story with the love and care it needs, thank you! I am so lucky to have two such wonderful editors on this book with me!

To my dear friends Elodie Harper and Jennifer Saint, this book wouldn't exist without your words of encouragement, your kindness, your generosity. I am blessed to know such brilliance as you!

To Micaela Alcaino, I could not have dreamed of a better cover designer and illustrator for this beautiful book – thank you for saying yes to this project and making such a glorious cover!

To the wonderful team at Simon & Schuster UK and the amazing team at Little Brown Young Readers, thank you so much for your hard work – it take a village to make a book come to life.

To all my fellow practitioners and daughters of Hekate – your guidance and love has made this reimagining stronger. Thank you.

With deepest gratitude to Sweety, Anita, Dean, Niall, Carlos, Yrsa, Costanza, Bea, Rowan, Natalie, Trista, Alison, Shaun, Rebekah, Clara, Annie, Emma, Heather, my parents and my brother.

And finally to you, dear reader. Thank you so much for entering the world of Hekate with me. Thank you for walking the lesser-known path and opening your heart to her story. Thank you. May joy and courage always find you where you are.